WASH YOU OFF MY SKIN

BY KING BENJAMIN

WASH YOU OFF MY SKIN Copyright © 2016 by King Benjamin.

Connect with King Benjamin:

Facebook: Author King Benjamin

Instagram: Author King Benjamin

This book is dedicated to the most important person in my life, my daughter Dalejah Deanna Jackson. I continue to strive to be all I can be because of you.

Acknowledgments

As always I have to give a big shout out to my DAA family. Authoress Kenya Rivers, India Norfleet, Danielle Marcus, and Lakelia Deloach-Lucas (Author BlackByrd). Love you all to death! Special shout out to my day one readers and supporters. I couldn't have done it without you guys. Special thanks to my homey Duke for pushing me and constantly encouraging me to pursue my God given talent as a career. Last, but certainly not least, I must thank God for giving me the strength and perseverance to follow through and weather every storm it took to get here.

Chapter 1

It was Marco's first day on the job. After serving three years in prison for drugs Marco was lucky to find a job as a laborer at a factory that built car seats for Ford Motor Company. He got the job because a friend he'd run into from his old neighborhood was a supervisor at the plant. He still felt awkward making the transition from the streets to the working world. The streets were all he knew, and this life was foreign, but he knew at this point it was the best decision he could make for his young life. At twenty-five years old his life still had potential, but he knew as a black man in America, and a convicted felon, his chances of making something of himself were decreasing by the day. He stood in the front of the lobby waiting for his friend to arrive, and show him to the time clock, and then his working area. His soon to be co-workers scurried in chatting amongst themselves and rushing off for last minute coffee runs. He notices the upbeat demeanor of the workers as they came off the streets and into the building, anxious to get the morning started.

He figured it a good sign that the people weren't disappointed to show up and work there. They were proud earners making decent money, unlike the desperate souls he was raised by. A few minutes passed before his friend Kevin showed up in the lobby with a bright smile on his face. Kevin was always a cool dude. He was a couple years older than Marco, but they were always cool since their preteen years. He could tell Kevin was glad to help out a friend in desperate need.

"Sup my dude?" Kevin spoke.

"Sup my nigga?" Marco spoke back as they slapped fives.

"Come on let me show you to the time clock," Kevin said.

As Kevin led the way to the main floor they pass the office cubicles where the main supervisors and the sales reps spent the majority of their time on the clock. They all looked extremely busy even though the day had just begun. When they reach the main floor, Marco could feel all the eyes on him as he and Kevin made their way to the main time clock.

"Now, I'm a tell you something about these guys in here. And when I say guys I really mean everybody, the men, and the women. They all nosy as hell and they gonna be in your business if you tell it to 'em. If I was you, I would chill to myself until I get a feel for the job, because all they do around here is gossip and keep bullshit up."

"I ain't tryna be involved in no drama. I need this job, you feel me?"

"I know you do, that's why I'm telling you what's up."

Kevin explained the punch in procedure and what was an acceptable starting time to show up and be punched in before he was considered late. As Kevin guided Marco across the floor to his work station, he could see men and women's necks stretched to capacity to get a glimpse of the new guy. He felt like an animal on display at the zoo. Right under six feet tall Marco was mocha brown with brush waves, and solid build from weight lifting the entire time he was incarcerated. He wore a shadow beard that he always kept neatly groomed. He landed at a workstation where a short woman with a huge backside stood by the assembly line waiting for the line to start up.

"Hey Kiara," Kevin greeted.

"Hey," Kiara spoke, then looked around the room as if to turn her attention away from the two of them.

"Kiara this is Marco. He gonna be working with you today. We gonna see how he does over here, and he might just be your partner."

"Oh okay," was all Kiara offered as she gave Marco a once-over and went back to scanning the rest of the floor as she slid her safety glasses over her face.

Kevin explained the details of Marco's job to him and he couldn't help but think the job seemed to be extremely easy. It was almost like he was missing the part where he would have to actually do some work. After explaining the break times and lunch options Kevin left Marco and Kiara alone to get started. Marco was a quality control inspector and he watched out for small but relevant mishaps on the assembly line. At first, it felt a little odd to be actually working at a real job. Marco was soaking up the experience as it was happening, so he wasn't cordial with his coworker Kiara at all. She seemed to be in a world of her own as well. As the first hour went rather quickly Kiara finally began to open up feeling her new coworker out.

"You and Kevin know each other from the streets?" Kiara asked.

"What make you say that?" Marco said.

"I just heard he was bringing one his friends in here to work with me."

"Oh yeah, when you hear that?"

"Friday," she announced, almost sounding proud that she stayed informed.

"Yeah, that's my mans, we from the same hood."

"Oh okay."

The two went at a steady pace throughout the next few hours. They would converse for five to ten minutes then work silently for another twenty. He learned Kiara was a twenty-seven-year-old single woman with no kids. She was barely over five feet tall, but he could tell she was a firecracker. Her voice was strong and forceful. The more he conversed with her, he decided she was at the very least a likable person and probably a nice coworker to work side by side with. Staring at her backside he couldn't help but drift off into lustful thought every now and again.

Marco was single, but he had a daughter that was born three months after he was incarcerated. She was his pride and joy and even though he wasn't with the mother, he tried his best to stay in good graces with her. Twelve noon came rather swiftly, and the break buzzer sounded overbearingly throughout the building. All of the line workers rushed to the break room or the parking lot. It was the first time Marco really got a chance to get a good look at a lot of his new coworkers up close. As they filed into the break room he was taking aback by the number of attractive women he saw roaming about chattering and laughing amongst themselves.

Friends quickly sectioned off in corners or took over entire areas of the break room. It was their routine, and he assumed they probably sat in the same areas every day. Marco had a lunch stored in one of many refrigerators lined along the back wall. His mother had made Sloppy Joe the night before and he was more than willing to help himself to the leftovers the next morning. He looked around for Kevin as he waited for his turn in one of four microwaves available in the break room. *Kevin probably went out for lunch, he thought.*

"You going in next?" a voice came from behind him.

He turned to put a face with the voice and was stunned by the beautiful specimen of a woman that stood before him. Even in work clothes and safety glasses resting on her forehead, he could tell that she was amazingly attractive. Her honey colored skin, her full reddish brown lips, and almond shaped eyes mesmerized him almost instantly.

"Huh?" he found himself mumbling.

"Are you going in there next? Cause she finished," the girl repeated for the second time, but this time offering a slight smile that was as alluring as the rest of her. Just then Marco realized he was daydreaming and holding up the microwave line.

"Damn, my bad," he commented as he moved closer to the microwave and began to removes his lunch from a zip-up lunch bag.

Once he was finished, Marco found a seat in a half empty section of the break room and began to chow down. He was never an overly friendly person, and he knew it would take him a minute to get to know the rest of the people he would be spending most of his days with. As he ate, he scanned the room for the pretty girl he had run into at the microwave. He quickly found her catty-corner to his right with her back turned to him, conversing with another slightly less attractive female. As if he had called her by name the girl turned around and looked in his direction. Their eyes locked momentarily before she turned back around and continued her conversation while enjoying lunch.

The remainder of the day was smooth and uneventful as Marco learned a little more about Kiara and vice versa. At the end of the day, Kevin offered Marco a ride home knowing he had taken public transportation to get there in hopes of finding a ride home after work. Marco gladly accepted and was more grateful than Kevin could image. It hurt his pride to stand at the bus stop with forty dollars to his name, but he was starting completely over after coming home to nothing but an open door at his mom's home. Marco's career as a criminal had been cut down in its prime, and after spending all of his money on lawyer fees, the little that was left he ran through it the first year of his incarceration. With a daughter to raise, he was willing to swallow his pride to be a consistent part of her life. As the two men rode the Davison freeway preparing to switch off on to the Lodge, Marco couldn't help but think about all of the women he had seen at the job he would love to have sex with. Only thirty days home he still hadn't had his first piece of pussy.

He hadn't tried to rekindle any old flames. He assumed the woman from his past would be expecting the old him. They wouldn't be too interested in the man he had become now, but deep down inside, he knew it was their loss, not his.

"Maaaaan, it's some fine muthafuckas up in that spot," Marco said.

"Oh yeah? You ain't seen nothing yet. It's even more on second shift," Kevin assured.

"What's up with 'em? They fucking?" Marco asked bluntly.

"Shiiiiid." Kevin shrugged. "If you get chose, I guess so. You got a lot of competition, I'll tell you that. These niggas be on everything new that come through the door. If they ain't married somebody probably already done tagged 'em," Kevin explained.

"Hmpt. Ain't that some shit. All I know is I need to fuck something fast. I been home thirty days today."

"You did good to find a job in thirty days my dude. Most dudes don't get that lucky."

"You right man, and I got you to thank for that. I ain't gon' never forget you showed me love on that one dog."

"I'm just glad I could help out. Where we grew up at, we didn't have a lot of options. I just got lucky enough to get out the streets before I got too caught up in it."

Kevin had dabbled in the streets hustling as a teen but he had quickly realized it wasn't the life for him. He found a job after high school and had been working ever since. As they pulled up to Marco's house he turned the music down just enough to make sure Kevin could hear him.

"Thanks for the ride dog," he said as he reached over and slapped fives with Kevin. "You know I ain't with that catching a bus shit so I gotta hurry up and get up on some cash for a whip."

"Well, you know I'll get you home if you can get there. I don't got a problem with taking you home, it's not too far out of my way anyway."

"Cool, cool, I'm a have to take you up on that. Oh, before I dipped... what's up with the one girl that works at the end of the line? Fine as hell with the long brown hair?"

"Ponytail?"

"Yeah, what's up with her?"

"Awe shit, that's Farrah. Don't even waste your time my dude," Kevin said shaking his head.

"Yeah?"

"Yeah. It ain't worth the chase," Kevin insisted.

"Alright," Marco said as the two parted ways.

Marco didn't need to know the specifics of why Farrah wasn't worth the chase. There were plenty more fish in that sea to choose from.

Chapter 2

When Marco made it home he raided his mom's fridge immediately. She came from her bedroom as soon she heard him in the kitchen. She smiled at his presence.

"How was work?" his mom asked.

"Good. It was good mama, how you feeling today?"

"I'm doing okay son."

Marco's mom needed two knee surgeries, but she was afraid to go under the knife. When her legs would swell up she was sometimes in great pain throughout the day. It always hurt Marco's heart to see her like that knowing wasn't much he could do. He was glad it wasn't one of those days.

"I'm starving mama," he announced.

"You ain't starving, you just greedy," she said shooing him with her hand. His mother Jeanine was in her mid-sixties and living off of her early retirement pension. It was really just enough to pay her monthly bills and afford the small luxury of cable television. Marco was thankful he lucked up and found a job making decent money. He wanted to help his mom out all he could, and he never wanted to resort back to the life from which he'd come. His mom made small talk as Marco rummaged through the kitchen cabinets looking for the hot sauce.

"You still ain't seen or heard from your brother?" Jeanine asked.

"Naw, I ain't heard from him," Marco replied.

Marco was had a brother eight years his senior. His name was Latrell, but everyone called him Trelly Well for reasons unknown. Trelly Well was addicted to drugs and his habits had force the majority of his family to turn their backs on him. He had crossed everyone including his own mother, stealing her money, putting her life in danger with outstanding drug debts in the neighborhood, not to mention the countless times her house had been raided with police looking for his whereabouts. But just like any other mother with a drug addicted son, she couldn't stop loving him. Even when she put him out on the streets she still sat up many nights wishing he would call. Nowadays she was just glad when she heard that he was still alive.

"If you see him out there somewhere, don't forget to tell him to call me."

"I will," Marco replied.

Unlike his mother, Marco didn't really care to see or hear from his older brother. Although he still loved his one and only brother, he felt like all the trouble he'd put Jeanine through, along with the overall disappointment he had turned out to be in life, it was probably just best they steered clear of each other. Marco knew he was no angel, but he was proud to say he was smartening up and making changes for the better with his life. After he ate Marco lounged around on the couch enjoying all the new television channels he didn't have access to up north. A few hours passed before the girl Farrah from his job popped in his head again from the out of the blue. He wished he knew more about her.

****

When Farrah made it home she only took a small break before she began the second part of her day. She needed to wash some clothes and make dinner for her boyfriend and their three-year-old son. At twenty-three, she had been with the same guy since the tenth grade in high school. He was tall and husky with peanut colored skin and a solid frame. Farrah loved Raheem, who was two years her senior and tried her best to keep him and her son happy all the time. She cooked and cleaned daily after work, and wasn't above getting out in the yard to cut grass or shovel snow if it needed to be done. Raheem was a good man, but after eight years he was comfortable and sometimes it bothered Farrah how monotonous the relationship had become. By the time Raheem made it home from work dinner was almost done. He walked in and tossed his keys on the coffee table then rubbed his son's head as he fell into the living room sofa in front of the TV.

"Sup li'l man?" Raheem said. "Sup," he repeated to Farrah as she passed through the hallway.

"Hey," she spoke.

That would be the highlight of their communication for hours to come. Raheem would get his food and settled in his man cave down in the basement, while Farrah played with her their son and washed dishes continuing to keep the house as clean as she could. Raheem Jr. was a mirrored image of his father, and when she looked into one's eyes she saw the other. They were the two men in her life that meant everything to her. Eventually, the two of them did have a pleasant conversation right before bedtime. Farrah liked to give her man his space, knowing he worked hard every day as a carpenter. The company he worked for was employed by a wealthy real estate investor. On the weekends he'd usually go hang out with his friends, and she'd either go visit her sister or grandmother. They lived a nice quite life and she wished they did more things together, but at the end of the day she was thankful just to have a drama free relationship with a man she could trust. After a nice relaxing shower Farrah finally turned in for bed after everyone else was fast asleep. It was just another regular day in Farrah's life. Tomorrow she would hit the floor at six am sharp and do it all over again.

Chapter 3

The next few days for Marco were a blur. The time moved so fast on the streets as opposed to being locked down all day with limited options and access to worldly things. Subconsciously, Marco feared letting his family down especially his daughter. So far, things were panning out. A week into the job, he made some more acquaintances and his relationship with his coworker Kiara flourished. She was now comfortable enough to share all of her personal business with him.

"Guess who like me?" Kiara said out of the blue, but it wasn't surprising. By now Marco had figured out Kiara thought she was hot stuff.

"Who?" Marco asked.

"Your boy Kevin," Kiara said proudly.

Almost every day Kiara claimed a different guy was in love with her. Marco never knew if she was overstating her popularity or not.

"Oh yeah? You like him?"

"He alright," Kiara said with a shrug as they continued to work side by side.

"Y'all should hook up," Marco suggested.

"I know he be talking about me, don't he?"

"He ain't say nothing to me about you, but ... you fine, I wouldn't be surprised," he flirted, feeding her ego just a nudge.

"We'll, I know the nigga make some good money, so you never know. We'll see," Kiara assured him.

Truth be told, Marco couldn't have cared less about Kiara's love life. He had his mind on Farrah because for some reason, every time this week he'd ran into her, he felt a strange connection to her without ever saying a word. Their eyes spoke volumes in a cryptic language.

That afternoon, as all the workers stepped with different strides on their way to the time clock Marco found himself walking directly behind Farrah. He couldn't help but enjoy the visual from behind. She wore throwback Jordans and skinny jeans that show off her heavenly assets, from her flawless legs to her round, plump backside. Her natural hair was wrapped in a ponytail that hung all the way down to the small of her back. Only a few steps behind her, Farrah could feel his eyes on her, and just like all the other times, she turned around and looked at him in his eyes. She didn't greet him with a smile nor did she give off any unwelcoming vibes. She just observed him as usual, and then continued on. In line at the time clock, they said nothing to each other standing almost side by side. Everyone talked around them, speaking of their plans for the weekend or complaining about the toll the work week had taking on them. Marco and Farrah just stood quietly taking small steps to their destination in unison. They simultaneously arrived at the time clock, but Marco was a gentleman and let her punch out first. He gestured for her to go ahead of him.

"You can go," she offered.

"Naw, ladies first."

Farrah took him up on his offer the second time and walked up to the clock and placed her hand on the scanner. Once she was punched out, instead of heading for the exit, she turned in the opposite direction. She appeared to be headed for the break room. After Marco was off the clock he headed in the same direction as Farrah. He always waited in the break room for Kevin to finish up detailing his boss about what had or hadn't been accomplished for the day. He was always alone in the break room while he waited, but today it looked like he may have company. Following up on his gentlemanly gesture at the clock, Marco decided to get the door for Farrah once he was sure he knew where she was going. He picked up his stride to make sure they arrived at the entrance at the same time.

"Let me get that for you," he offered grabbing the break room door.

"Thank you," Farrah replied.

"Ain't nothing."

The two walked into the empty room and only the noise of their movement could be heard. They took seats at opposite ends of the first picnic style lunch table. Marco was the first to end the silence.

"TGIF", he said as he made eye contact with her.

"Yes, thank God," Farrah agreed. "I'm sooooo tired."

She rolled her neck around and slightly massaged it for emphasis.

"Yeah, me too. It's an easy job, but standing on your feet all day is what wears you down."

"Right, cause I be seeing you and Kiara over there, and y'all don't be doing no work," she teased.

Her smile lit up the room.

"What? You crazy! You tryna say we don't work at our station?"

"I'm just joking," she admitted.

After the short icebreaker, the two went back to their individual thoughts, and the room fell silent again. Farrah didn't like the silence either.

"You waiting on your ride?" Farrah asked.

"Yeah. My man Kevin drops me off every day. What about you? You waiting on a ride?"

"Yeah, my car is in the shop."

"What's wrong with it?"

"They said it's the ball bearings, ball joints, ball something," she giggled.

"That's how y'all women are; I swear y'all don't care what the problem is, just fix it, and give me my shit back in working order."

"Exactly," she said pointing in his direction. "I'm just glad it's payday."

"For you maybe," Marco commented.

"Oh yeah, this your first week, so you don't get paid until next week right?"

"Hell yeah."

"Sorry," she said poking out her lip for no reason.

"It's cool. I'm just glad to have a job."

"I know that's right. So you like it here?"

"Yeah, it's cool I..."

Just then Farrah's cell phone rang putting a pause on the conversation. At the same time, Kevin entered the break room and signaled for Marco. Kevin looked at Farrah who was also preparing to leave out then back at Marco. Farrah tucked her cell phone away in her purse and headed out the door. The three wound up all heading for the exit together, with Farrah leading the pack. The two men watched from behind as her ass jiggled a little with every step.

"Mmp mmp mmp," Marco said loud enough for only the two of them to hear it.

"Don't waste your time my dude. I'm trying to tell you." Kevin insisted.

"Yeah... I hear ya."

****

Since Raheem was still at work, Farrah had to bum a ride with her sister Fatima. From Farrah's job they rode straight to the daycare center to pick up her son. Farrah strapped him into the car seat that was usually designated for Fatima's son who was around the same age.

"Heeeey Raheem," Fatima squealed from the driver's seat staring back at her nephew.

"He mad," Farrah said explaining the discontent look plastered across Raheem Jr.'s face.

"What he made about?"

"I don't know. I'm still trying to find out. Why you mad Raheem?" Farrah asked climbing back into the passenger seat.

His face showed extreme dissatisfaction with the current situation.

"I ain't get no canny," he explained.

"What? You ain't get no candy?" Farrah asked.

"Yeah. I ain't get no canny," he repeated.

"Why you ain't get none? They was passing out candy and ain't give you none?"

"I drop my canny on the floor.

"Oooh, you dropped your candy and they didn't have anymore?"

"Yeah," he grunted.

"Don't worry about it baby, mama will stop and get you something before we get home."

Five minutes before Farrah reached her sanctuary the automotive repair shop called and told her that her car was ready. Her sister drove her to the shop to pick it up. As the radio blasted an old Ashanti and Ja Rule song, her mind drifted back to the new guy at work. He was cute and seemed like a cool guy. She couldn't help but notice his muscular frame hidden underneath the work kakis and matching shirt. Farrah was a good girl and never had a wandering eye for the majority of her eight-year relationship, so she dismissed her observations as nothing more than that.

"What you got planned for the weekend?" Fatima asked.

Farrah shook her head.

"Nothing. Girl you know I don't got no life," she admitted as the pulled into the parking lot of the shop.

"I'll come over and have a drink with you tomorrow if you want."

"Might as well," Farrah said in a nonchalant tone.

"Shit, you ain't gotta say it like that. I could keep my money and go find somebody to drink with that like my company," Fatima complained.

The two sisters were only a few years apart and grew up very close. Fatima being the oldest she was the first to have sex, the first to have a child -her six-year-old daughter- and the first to move out of their parent's home. Farrah learned a lot about life watching her older sister live it first. She learned from her good as well bad decisions. At twenty-three and twenty-six they were both proud of each other for becoming responsible adults and good parents. They'd had their share of obstacles growing up.

Farrah picked up her Jeep Liberty that was midnight blue with peanut butter interior. It was a little dusty on the outside from being in the shop the past two days. It wasn't long before she pulled away from the shop that Raheem Jr. had fallen asleep in his car seat. She decided to run her car through the automatic carwash near her home. After a quick wash, her jeep was sparkling like it just left the showroom floor. The sun was shining brightly on a warm mid-spring day, and she couldn't help but feel a little bothered by the fact that she was probably about to park her pretty truck in the driveway where it would more than likely sit for the next two days until it was time to returned to work Monday morning.

Chapter 4

Marco promised to spend some time with his daughter when the weekend came around. That Saturday morning Nae, the mother of his child, was at his doorstep bright and early to drop her off. His mother Jeanine was in the kitchen frying up a breakfast fit for a king, with eggs, turkey bacon, pancakes and cheese grits. When the doorbell rung Marco was still in his pajamas as he waltzes to the door. He opened the door and there was his beautiful daughter Mariah, standing there cheesing from ear to ear. He could sense her delight to be finally getting to spend some time with him. She didn't know what to expect, but she knew it was going to be a new and exciting experience. They hadn't seen much of each other in the past three years, except on photos taken in hopes of capturing what no amount of words could convey. The first time Marco laid eyes on his five-year-old daughter, he knew he'd made the right decision to change his course. Every time since then their reunion was reaffirming.

"Come on," Marco said as he opened the door for Nae and Mariah then stepped aside.

"Hey," Nae spoke.

"What up," he replied.

The two hadn't spoken much outside of discussing their plans of co-parenting and setting dates and times for Marco to get Mariah. Mariah was very familiar with the house, and when she smelt the food cooking she went flying off to the kitchen to find her grandmother.

"Ooooooooh, there go my Stinka!" they heard Jeanine yell out.

While Jeanine continued to woo Mariah, Marco and Nae sat down in the living room.

24

"How you been?" Marco asked.

"Better, now that you home to give me some help," Nae said.

Marco thought it wasn't the best way to start off a conversation, but he brushed it off.

"That I am," he replied.

"Good. That reminds me, she needs some shoes."

"Won't have no real bread until next week. I don't get paid until next Friday."

"I know. I'm just saying..."

"I'll take care of it."

Nae still had her looks intact. Becoming a mother had only filled her out a little more in the right places. She was five-six, caramel with full lips and a nice grade of naturally wavy hair. If Marco thought he could get away with smashing her without all the drama to come afterward, he'd be all over her like flies to shit. But all the battle scars hadn't healed and he didn't want to risk opening old wounds.

"So what y'all doing today?" Nae said.

"We just went hang out and chill. Can't do too much, I ain't got no bread like that."

"It's nice outside, she not gonna want to sit up in the house."

"Well, what can I do Nae? I don't have a car, and I just told you I don't get paid until next week."

"You can use my car. Take her to the park or something," Nae suggested.

Marco was skeptical. He wondered where the punch line was.

"You gon' let me borrow your car?" He asked for clarity.

"Yeah. I trust you, especially if you got my daughter with you. And you already know better than to have some bi..."

Just then Jeanine and Mariah came strolling in the living room putting a pause on the conversation. Marco was glad.

"Nae you want some breakfast baby?" Jeanine asked.

"I'm okay, thanks; me and Mariah just ate breakfast."

"Nae said she gon' let me use her car today. You believe her mama?" Marco said with his lips curled in skepticism.

"Mmm Hmm. And you better not have no fast tail ass women up in her car either," Jeanine said.

"Wooooow. Really? You just gon' pick a side that fast huh mama?"

"I ain't picking no damn sides. I'm telling you what bet not happen."

"That's right mama," Nae said.

It was odd to hear Nae still calling his mother, 'mama' as if they were still all one big family. Throughout all the ups and downs, Jeanine and Nae maintained their relationship. Had it not been for Marco's, street life and promiscuity, there was a huge possibility the two would have reconciled before it got too ugly. The way he saw things now they would never fall in love again, but he would always love her.

As promised, Nae allowed Marco to drop her off at a friend's house while he kept her silver Pontiac Grand Prix. When Marco and Mariah pulled off together he glanced in the review and he could see she was still sporting a slight smile, filled with expectations. He drove to Bell Isle Park on Jefferson, knowing his daughter would thoroughly enjoy the scenery when they drove over the bridge that sat perched right over the Detroit River. Seagulls glided through the air hovering near a rapidly moving speed boat, as the light traffic on the bridge move at a steady pace. When they reached the entrance of the park Marco turned the radio down to a whisper.

"So what you wanna do li'l mama? You wanna go to the swings or something?"

"Yeah...I wanna go," Mariah answered.

"We on our way then."

Mariah stared wide-eyed out the window scoping out any and every activity taking place around her. There was a family picnic going on and she saw a lot of kids running around. Motorcycle clubs zoomed past on their big loud bikes. In the middle of the strip, Marco pulled over and parked near the swings. After unfastening her car seat, Marco picked Mariah up and began to carry her across the grass to the play area. There were only a couple other kids hanging out at the swings, along with their parents. One little girl seemed to be enjoying both parents pushing her back and forth as she swung to the highest of heights attainable. Then there was a little boy and his mom. The closer Marco got, the more the mom looked extremely familiar. He only had to take a few more steps to realize the young mom was Farrah from his job. He couldn't believe out of all the people in the world to run into, here she was.

After their short conversation in the break room on Friday, he'd found it hard to shake the thought of her. The minute Farrah looked up and noticed him she waved and smiled. Marco strolled over with his daughter in his arms.

"Small world huh?" Marco said.

"You know the D is a small world anyway. How you doing?"

Farrah's banging five-five frame was on display in a sexy black sundress.

"I'm good, how you doing?"

"Good, just out here enjoying this nice day. Is this your daughter?"

"Yeah, this my li'l mama. Is that your son?"

"Yeah, this my bad ass," she said with a giggle.

"He don't look bad at all," Marco commented.

"Shiiiiid. His ass drove me crazy at terrible two."

The two kids looked on curiously at each other while the parents continued to talk. Since the swing next to Farrah was unoccupied, Marco put Mariah in the swing as she and Raheem Jr. continued to feel each other out with their eyes. "What's her name?" Farrah asked.

"Mariah."

"Hey Mariah," Farrah said waving and Mariah waved back.

"What's your son name?"

"Raheem Bad Ass is what we like to call him."

They both giggled before Marco spoke to Raheem, who just looked without responding as his swing began to slow down, almost to a halt, because his mom was engaging some man instead of pushing him.

"Mama!" Raheem complained.

Farrah went to stand behind the swing and push Raheem and Marco did the same for Mariah. For some reason, Farrah was glad to see Marco and felt comfortable in his presence. After thinking the weekend over in her head, Farrah decided she would do her best to try and get out of the house and enjoy her off days. After double checking with her man about his plans, she was certain he was not going to take her anywhere and do anything with her. She had grown used to the distance between them and just assumed that this was the way most couples lived after being together for a lengthy period. The two things Farrah love about Raheem was that he was a great provider and an even better lover. She couldn't remember the last time he'd brought her anything, but whatever the house needed, he either fixed it or paid for it.

"So how you like the job so far?" Farrah asked.

"I like it. The work is pretty easy, and it pays decent so... what more could you ask for?"

"A raise," Farrah answered. "These gas prices ain't no joke."

"I know, that shit is crazy. Gas was already going up before I went away but now that shit is like woah!"

"Went away?" Farrah said as her curiosity rose.

"Yeah, I been locked up for the past few years. I only been home for a month and some change," Marco informed.

"So you a thug?" Farrah teased with a slight smile.

Mariah began to giggle uncontrollably as she went flying high in the air.

"Naw, I was a hustler. I guess you could be both at the same time, but I never claimed to be one."

"One what?"

"A thug."

"I'm just messing with you. So you learned your lesson?"

"You see where I'm at every day, don't you?"

"Ha! Yeah, I guess that answers that. Them street ain't it though foreal. Two of my cousins got killed trying to be all out there."

"Yeah... some shit you just gotta learn on your own, you know?"

"Right," Farrah agreed.

By now Marco was beginning to notice how comfortable Farrah was with him and it boosted his confidence level towards the conversation. Kevin's words replayed in the back of his mind making him hesitant at the same time.

"How long you been with the company?" Marco asked.

"Since I was nineteen so, like four years."

She was around the same age he'd predicted her to be in his head.

Marco became engulf in her beauty for a moment. He couldn't remember the last time he'd saw a woman that was that gorgeous so effortlessly. She wore the same high ponytail and some black open toe sandals that showed off her pedicured toes. Her flawless skin and glowing features just made here eye candy to everyone she crossed paths with man or woman.

"You know you really something to look at," Marco admitted.

Farrah smiled shyly.

"Thank you," Farrah said, but she was really thinking, *you're not bad yourself,* even though she didn't dare say it aloud.

Marco looked up and noticed three women headed in his direction. He peered in closer with his head cocked to the side as he began to recognize all of them. It was Nae and two of her friends.

"Come here Marco," Nae called out, fingering him in.

He let Mariah continue to swing while he walked the short distance and cut off Nae's path to the swings. The look on her face read she wasn't a happy camper at the moment.

"You supposed to be spending time with your daughter, why is you out here chatting with hoes? Who is that?" Nae asked.

"Girl if don't get the fuck on, I am spending time with my daughter."

"Yeah, it looks like you spending time with your daughter, some bitch, and somebody's son."

Farrah looked on watching Nae's neck rolling. She couldn't hear every word being spoken, but she could definitely tell it was pertaining to her and Marco.

"You sound stupid as hell. You just came all the way out here to watch what the fuck I'm doing?"

"No, I just happening to be riding by and saw your sneaky ass. We already had plans to come to the park."

"Sneaky how?"

"So you not with that bitch in my car?"

"In your car? That's my new coworker, we just happened to be in the same place at the same fucking time," Marco explained.

This is why he knew beyond a shadow of a doubt that he and Nae would never be good together. Here he was explaining himself for having a simple conversation with someone that just happened to be a beautiful woman. It reminded him of her flawed personality traits that he'd overlooked during the stent of their relationship. Sometimes he felt she drove him to cheat by constantly accusing him. Either way, he had ruined her trust and couldn't get it back.

"All I know is I better not catch you with no bitch in my car."

"You know what? You ain't even gonna have to worry about that, because soon as we leave from here, you will have your car right back. I'll find a way home."

Marco walked away from Nae and went back to the swings. Nae wanted to continue her rant, but Marco was no longer a willing participant in the feud, so she and her friends turned to leave. All Marco could think of was that he had to hurry up and get his shit together because the last thing he needed was Nae thinking he depended on her for anything.

****

The mood was ruined after Marco's altercation with Nae and Farrah left the park with her son shortly after. As soon as he left the park Marco called Nae to find out her whereabouts and take her car back. She didn't answer. He called several times and the phone just rang. He was positive she was ignoring his calls to get back at him for whatever she was upset about. Nae had a mean jealous streak since as far back as he could remember. It started off kind of cute to him, but through the four years, they were together it caused a lot of unwanted drama. For a while, he drove around aimlessly with the music low, contemplating and waiting for Nae to return his call. He wound up back in his neighborhood and he stopped at the party store to get Mariah some snacks. As he helped his young daughter from the back seat of the car, Marco looked up and spotted his brother Trelly Well had popped out on the corner, in front of the store. It was the first time he'd seen Trelly Well in years and he looked bad; real bad. His brother was looking in every direction but behind him, and still hadn't notices Marco approaching.

"Trelly Well," he called out.

Trelly Well turned to see his brother and niece walking hand in hand in his direction. The smile that spread across his face was dingy but genuine.

"Whussup baby bro? Awe man I heard you was home my nigga," he said as he reached out to hug his brother.

Marco embraced him and was quickly overtaken by his brother's strong body order. He was way below his normal weight and he hadn't shaved or cut his hair in months.

"Bro I see you still out here on the bullshit huh?" Marco said.

"Hey my beautiful niece. Hey Mariah, it's your uncle Trelly Well," his brother pretended not to hear him and continued to familiarize Mariah with who he was. "It's your uncle Trelly... you remember me don't you?"

Mariah shook her head no.

"Man, you look bad bro. And you need to go see your mama and let her know you still alive."

"I know... I know. I'm a call mama soon as I get to a phone."

Marco reached into his pocket and grabbed his cellphone.

"Here. The number still the same. And don't take off with my phone either, I'll be right back," Marco warned as he took Mariah inside the party store. A few minutes later Marco returned with a bag full of goodies for Mariah, who was still clueless as to who exactly Trelly was.

"Somebody trying to call you baby bro," Trelly said handing him his phone back.

"Hello?" Marco answered.

"Yeah," he heard Nae's voice say.

"Where you at?"

"I'm at home. Why?"

"Stay there, I'm on my way."

Marco hung up and prepared to leave from the corner that Trelly obviously was about to hang out on for a while and do God knows what. "Trelly where you staying man?"

"I'm around. Just come over Laureen house if you need to find me."

Marco shook his head and walked off wondering was his brother a lost cause. Right now it didn't much matter because he had a kid to raise and a mom to look after. Trelly would have to figure it out on his own.

****

As he drove to Nae, Mariah fell fast asleep in her car seat. When Marco arrived at Nae's home she had left the front door open with the storm door locked. He looked around inside for her as he rang the bell. Nae appeared in the doorway wearing a different outfit than the one she had worn earlier in the day. Now she wore a tight-fitted multicolored print dress with black peep toe heels.

"We need to talk," Marco said as he came inside carrying Mariah, who was still asleep in his arms.

"You right, we do. You can lay her down in her bed," Nae said.

Marco lay Mariah down and when he came back to the living room Nae was brushing her hair in front of the small vanity with a metal trim that hung near the foyer. Her back was turned to him and he couldn't help but notice her ass. He didn't want to, but there it was staring him right in the face and looking tempting as can be.

"Listen, I don't ever want to use your car again because I don't need know drama from you. We need to have a good relationship for Mariah's sake."

"Marco I don't care about that car, it's just the point that I know how you is. Some stuff never changes, and I don't want you to try and make me out to be the extra jealous, drama filled bitch, just because I stopped to make sure you didn't have a bitch in my car."

"If that's not drama, what do you call it? Look, what's done is done, never mind that. But moving forward, we gotta be adults about this shit. A lot have changed about me rather you believe it or not. That's why I'm not fucking with none of them no good hoes from my past."

"Yeah right," Nae said and she stood in front of him with both hands on her hips.

"Yeah right what?"

"So you not fucking with none of them brauds you was fucking before you went to jail?"

"Naw, I'm not. What I gotta lie to you for?"

Suddenly, Nae had a strange sparkle in her eyes.

"So who you fucking?"

"Honestly? Nobody."

"Mmm Hmm. Let me see," Nae said as she took a few seductive steps invading his personal space before meeting him with a bold kiss in the mouth. Marco wanted to resist her advance, but couldn't think of a good reason to at the moment. Her lips, her scent and the warmth of her body up against his were enough to make his soldier rise at attention. After all, she was his baby mama and someone he used to really love. With a second kiss, all the hormonal build up that he had been pushing to the back of his mind came rushing to the front. Nae stroked his jeans in the front to see if her seduction was working. Even though she hadn't decided if she wanted to be with Marco or not, she wanted to be damn sure she was his first option. The thought of him really moving on did something to her. Marco only had plans to co-parent, but when he slid his arms around her waist and then let them drop

35

down to grip her nice juicy bottom; he knew that it would be a lot easier said than done.

"You really wanna start something huh? After all we been through?" Marco said as he continued to hold her in his arms and get reacquainted with her body.

"So what, I got first dibs on this dick," she said as she stroked him.

Marco couldn't help but grin knowing he wanted to fuck just as much as she did. "Now come on up these steps before Mariah wake up or I change my mind."

Marco did as he was told, but as he ascended the stairs his joyful lust was slightly distracted by the possible indications and repercussion of his actions. He hoped for the best and prepare for the worst. That's how he had always lived his life.

Chapter 5

Farrah and Raheem made good love Sunday morning. It had become somewhat of a ritual for them to have sex every Saturday night and Sunday morning. Throughout the work week, it seemed one or the other was too tired or too distracted to make any sexual advances. After he'd showered and dressed, Raheem seemed to distance himself from her most of the day hanging out in his man cave, but he did spend time with his son. Farrah lay in bed watching Lifetime Network and talking on the phone with the only real friend she had, her sister. She had many associates but no friends. Sometimes she wished she had more friends, but the drama that came along with constant female interaction just wasn't worth it. Guys were so much easier to get along with, but Raheem had long ago chased all of her male friends away.

Raheem could be extremely jealous at times, but because Farrah lived such a low-key lifestyle she didn't give him much reason to distrust her. As her mind wandered off, the thought of Marco came from thin air. She reflected on the scene at the park and was baffled when she heard the small voice in her head say *'I can't fuck with him anyway, his baby mama seems crazy'.* What?

Where the fuck did that come from? She thought. Farrah was not an unhappy woman and didn't have a wandering eye. She brushed it off as the devil at work and went down to the man cave with her favorite men. She spent the rest of her evening enjoying her family.

****

Monday afternoon Marco and Farrah found themselves in the lunch room again waiting on a ride after work. This time, Raheem's car was going in the shop, so he took Farrah to work and drove her car. It seemed Marco and Farrah were constantly being forced together by chance. They were the only people there and the two stood face to face having a conversation that really held Farrah's attention. They had so much in common. She didn't know if it was his sexy vocal tone or the fact that he felt so familiar that had her at complete attention whenever Marco talked. Whatever it was she enjoyed it.

"I ain't gon' lie, you the most beautiful thing I laid eyes on in a minute," Marco said changing subjects.

Farrah blushed uncontrollably.

"Whaaaaat? I sure don't feel like that," Farrah said honestly. "I'm just a regular chick."

"Nah that's where you wrong. Ain't nothing regular about you. I know you probably got a man at home that won't let you out of his sight, don't you?"

"I do," Farrah nodded innocently but ate up the compliments.

"Oh yeah?" Marco said as he stepped in a little closer invading her space.

"Yeah," Farrah admitted in an almost disappointed tone.

"What if I told you I was gon' take you from that nigga?" Marco said as he moved in even closer and wrapped both arms around Farrah's waist.

"I would say you crazy," Farrah responded, but then realized his arms were around her waist and she wasn't doing anything about it. Why wasn't she doing anything about it? What possessed him to think he had the right to touch her? "Umm, I think you should move your hands," she finally said.

Marco looked down into her eyes and smiled with his confidence completely intact.

"You think so? You sure you really want that?"

Before Farrah could answer Marco leaned in and kissed her softly. He kissed her again and both times, Farrah enjoyed the tastes of his lips. The third kiss was not a peck, but a French one that made Farrah lose her will to resist at all. She lapped his tongue with her own, and all of a sudden the lunch room door came open and the two broke their kiss and jumped back away from each other startled by the intrusion. It was Kevin, and when he walked in, he looked more dazed and confused than even Marco and Farrah.

Farrah was jolted from her dream and sat straight up in her bed until her reality and surroundings began to surface clearly. She took a deep breath as she tried to make sense of such a ridiculous dream. If a man ever touched her without her consent he'd get an open-handed slap in the mouth, amongst other things. She turned to look down at Raheem who was fast asleep. She lay back down and snuggled up next to him thinking maybe she should make her way to the house of the Lord soon because the devil was really working on her lately.

Chapter 6

After Marco and Nae had sex, Marco gain access to Nae's car keys on a regular basis. Their schedules allowed Marco to drop her off at work, and pick her up, with only a small wait from the time Nae got off. It was a much better deal than public transportation, but Marco was saving for his own vehicle knowing things could blow up in his face with Nae at any moment. For the time being, they were getting along great and even though he saw trouble brewing in the future he stuck to his rule; hope for the best and prepare for the worst. Marco made enough money each week to establish a bank account, piece together a new wardrobe, and provide for his daughter.

Meanwhile, his relationships at work continued to flourish. He was very well liked amongst all his coworkers and thought to be easygoing and charismatic. While he and Nae figured things out he took the opportunity to get to know all of the single women at the job since he spent so much of his time there. Sadly enough, the only real connection he felt was to a woman who was already attached. Marco and Farrah enjoyed each other's company and their chemistry was undeniable every time they crossed paths. Their hellos and goodbyes led to lengthy conversations, which led to the revelations of all the things they had in common. They shared the same love for music, books and trying new things. Marco had sold drugs as a youth, while Farrah watched her mom battle a drug addiction that left her without clothes to wear to school at times.

As the two grew closer, Marco began to understand that Farrah's ties to the hood struggle and her burning desire for a better life is what made their connection so real. Marco always wanted for a better life and as

Farrah began to open up to him, he reciprocated the same. It was obvious to all of their coworkers that the two had become friends, but there was nothing out of the ordinary about their relationship. That was all about to change.

"Happy birthday homey," Marco said as he took a seat at the lunch table across from Farrah.

Farrah wore a tight-fitting T-shirt that read, *It's My Birthday* across the front. It had about seventy-five dollars pinned to her left breast as her coworkers had been generously showing her birthday love throughout the day. It was a warm day in June and almost everyone had decided to go out for lunch.

"Thanks my good friend," Farrah replied as she looked around the lunch room noticing how vacant it was. Only two other people in such a spacious room seemed like a rare occasion. "Why you ain't go out for lunch?" Farrah said smiling and glad she wasn't going to have to eat alone.

"I wanted to come kick it with you since today is your birthday and all. I'm surprised you didn't take the day off and chill," Marco said as he took in her overwhelming beauty.

"You know I don't got no life. What I'm gonna do stay home and sleep?" Farrah giggled.

"I don't know. Don't you and your boyfriend got have plans?"

"Not really. We going out to eat but that's about it."

"Hmpt. Anyway, I got you something," Marco said as he removed a small package from his windbreaker pocket. Marco had thought it over for a few days and decided he wanted to give Farrah something for her birthday. It was and unselfish act that he was hoping would solidify their friendship. He enjoyed her. He knew she was taken, but she was obviously feeling a connection as well. Whatever she had to offer he welcomed it, and his secret lust for her was growing quicker than he realized. He slid the small rectangular box across the table to Farrah. "Happy birthday," he repeated.

At first, Farrah just eyed the box suspiciously, before meeting eyes with Marco.

"I can't be taking strange gifts from other men," she said as she smiled and glanced around the room to see if anyone was watching.

"So you telling me all that money on your titties came from women?" Marco question as Farrah burst into laughter.

"That's different, but what is this in this box?" Farrah asked as she tapped the box three times.

"It's not nothing major, it's just a little something to make to your birthday just that much better that's all. Don't read nothing into it, just open it."

Farrah gave him a skeptical glance, but then went ahead and opened the box. Inside was small costume jewelry bracelet made of big black ovals. It only cost Marco twenty-five dollars, but he figured it was the thought that counted, and he was right.

"This is soooo sweet of you," Farrah said as her face lit up while she pulled the bracelet out of the box and took it into her hands. Once Farrah saw the bracelet, she knew she was going to keep it because she liked it too much to give it back. *Besides its just costume jewelry, she told herself.*

"You like it?" Marco said, but knowing the answer.

"I do. Thank you, I'm gonna wear this a lot too."

"Good, I'm glad you like it. Now put it away before the wrong person sees it and starts spreading rumors," Marco said with a chuckle.

"Right," Farrah agreed putting her gift back in the box and tucking it away. "This don't mean we dating or nothing," Farrah said with a smile.

Marco didn't know if it was a joke or her making a serious clarification, but he laughed it off anyway.

"Who said something about dating? You got a man and I got a situation. We just cool like that you know?"

"Right," Farrah replied still all smiles but trying to figure Marco out. It was highly unlikely that he didn't have some kind of ulterior motive, but he wasn't like any of the other men she'd came in contact with over the years she'd been at her job. They had all tried to get into her panties and failed miserably, but Marco felt different; more sincere and just... real. "I hope you mean that."

It felt good to Farrah to have a male friend she could talk to, and her attraction to him made each conversation just that much spicier and intriguing. But staring into her beautiful brown eyes Marco knew that he would eventually want a lot more than her conversation if they continued down this road. He knew he would much rather travel this road and see where it led them than to take the high road.

"I do mean it. Even though I do got a little thing for you, I won't front about that. Some stuff you just can't act on."

"You starting to really grow on me too," Farrah admitted. Her trust level with Marco was slowly growing and he could see the change.

Something told Marco he needed to seize the opportunity to strengthen the bond he was creating while her guard was down.

"So listen. I'm thinking you should take my number down," he ventured.

"For what?" Farrah asked confused.

"You know... in case you just ever want to talk to me about anything."

"You trying to get me killed?"

"Nah...I'm just trying to make sure you have the option to reach me if you ever wanted to when we wasn't at work."

He thought he was so smooth with his game he was running. Farrah knew it was game, but something made her play along anyway because... well, it was fun.

"I think you trying to make a move," she giggled taking in his sexy frame and lips.

"Maaaan. See that's your problem, you think too much. Just take the number down and lock it in under a girl name or something and then we'll be good."

Farrah sat back in her chair and the two went into the strangest stare off as they sat grinning at each other for about ten seconds, before Farrah slid her phone across the table to Marco.

"Don't make me regret this," Farrah said.

Marco dialed his number into Farrah's IPhone and slid it back to her.

"You won't ever regret nothing about me," he promised.

Chapter 7

A couple months passed and Marco never received a single call or text from Farrah. Their relationship continued to develop over the hours they spent working together, but it seemed to flatline every day when they punched time cards and went their separate ways. Farrah invaded Marco's thoughts more and more, but he continued to push her to the back of his mind. As bad as he wanted her, he wasn't willing to chase a woman that was in a confirmed, committed relationship. Still, he couldn't help but daydream sometimes about her long, flowing hair, the beauty mark that sat perched right on top of those luscious lips; the small waist that was attached to such thickness that she carried in her hips, thighs, and ass.

The time Marco spent with Nae kept his body busy, but his mind was constantly on Farrah. The ball was in her court now, and he knew she was a smart girl. Farrah knew a phone call to him would give Marco the confidence to overstep the set boundaries of their friendship. He found himself longing for the day she would call. By now he was convinced she wanted him just as much as he did her. It was in her eyes every time they spoke and every day he could sense her need to be near him. Today was a big day for Marco. He had finally saved up enough money to make a trip to the car lot. He wanted to make a sizable down payment to make sure his monthly note wasn't too high.

Even as he roamed the car lot with his eyes scanning the entire area, Farrah was still lingering around in the back of his mind. He wanted a car that would impress her. Make her see him as somebody with a bright future. He hadn't laid a hand on her, but here he was making her a part of his buying options and decision process. His eyes landed on a late model black on black Suburban. It was a truck he really couldn't afford, but he wanted it anyway. It was something that would make him feel good about himself and better about his decision to leave the game. If he could still manage to have nice things without risking life a limb, he could then consider himself truly blessed.

****

Farrah sat at home alone on another boring Saturday afternoon. Her son was away with her sister and her man was somewhere avoiding her, or at least that's what it felt like. She had suggested they go see a movie, but instead, he was working on a project that could have waited until Monday. She knew once he finished working he would probably come home, shower, change and leave out again. For the first time, she was starting to question was Raheem being unfaithful to her. Even if he wasn't, he definitely wasn't living up to his boyfriend duties as of lately. She could barely get a twenty-minute conversation with him when she had this dude Marco who seemed to always know what to say. Marco always had time for her and always made her feel important. He listened when she talked, and he was even wise enough to give her sound advice when she needed it.

Farrah valued their friendship and as the days went by it became harder and harder to resist the temptation to pick up her phone and call him, just to see what he sounded like over the phone. She told herself she was being childish, but in her heart of hearts, she knew Marco was slowly seeping his way inside her chest. On this particular day, her boredom just became too much to bear and she found herself contemplating making the call. *If she made the call it didn't mean anything. It didn't have to lead to anything else.*

Nothing would happen unless she allowed it to, she told herself. Before she could change her mind Farrah went to the window and peeked out of the blinds to make sure Raheem wasn't pulling up outside. She sighed deeply then scrolled through her contacts until she found Marco's number. As the phone rang, she wondered was he with Nae? *Should she just hang up the phone right now? What if Nae answered the phone?* She was about to just hung up, but before she could, Marco's voice came through the speaker.

"Hello?"

"Can I speak to Marco?"

"Speaking, who this?"

"Farrah, are you busy?"

"Who?" Marco said honestly in shock.

"This is Farrah, are you busy?"

"Oh really? I mean, nah I'm not busy. I'm just leaving the car lot."

Marco felt a rush of adrenaline flow through his body as he drove down the main street leaving the car lot with his brand new truck, while he talked on his cell phone to the woman who had begun to haunt him in his dreams. It was something about her that just made life feel better.

"You bought a car?" Farrah said ready to get excited for him.

"A truck," Marco responded.

"Yaaaaaay! We got us a truck," she teased and giggled.

"Ha... ain't no we got a truck, I got a truck. You know you ain't gon' never see the inside of it, unless you peek inside from the parking lot."

Farrah laughed off the comment but didn't offer one in return. It was what she did every time there was even the slightest potential for their conversation to veer into uncharted territory.

"Sooo whassupper?" Farrah finally said as she felt her mood instantly changing the moment they began conversing. Marco always seemed to be there for her. He was caring and dependable along with all the other great qualities he had. It was too bad they were already in situations.

Farrah and Marco would spend the next two hours on the phone talking about everything from high school to kids and relationships. It was by far the longest conversation they'd ever had and each person knew much more about the other than they'd ever known previously. They could talk about anything privately without nosey coworkers around. It was a beautiful day outside and Farrah sat on her front porch taking in the rays of sunshine, while throwing her head back in fits of laughter, as Marco tickled her mental funny bone. Every once in a while she'd glance up and down the street at the cars coming and going, making sure Raheem didn't creep up on her.

"I'm glad you finally call me," Marco admitted.

"I'm glad I did too. You know... I never had a male friend like you."

"Well, I think I can say the same thing. I never had a female friend like you," Marco replied truthfully.

"You don't mean that."

"The hell if I don't. Now you and I both know that I haven't laid a finger on you, but somehow I found myself growing more and more attached to you."

"Attached?"

"Yeah, you know, connected."

"Oh yeah, same here," Farrah confessed as she looked up the street and spotted Raheem's Charger about to pull in their driveway. "Hey, I gotta go okay?"

"Okay, I'll see you Monday."

"See you Monday."

Just as Farrah was ending the call Raheem was getting out his car and approaching the front porch. It wasn't the smoothest timing in the world and Farrah felt like the guilt was written all over her face.

"Why you get off the phone when I roll up?" Raheem asked in a nonchalant tone.

"Because my conversation was over," she plainly stated.

"Whatever. That was boyfriend number two," he teased as he bypassed her and went inside the house.

Farrah didn't respond to his slick comments because she was too busy trying to figure out was there any truth to the statement. *Did she really have another boyfriend on the side? Technically, was she already cheating by letting Marco get so close to her?* Deep down inside, she knew any relationship she had to hide from her man wasn't right, but Marco filled a need that she could not put a finger on. For some strange reason, whatever it was he was offering she wanted to see what it led to.

Chapter 8

One month later

After his ninety-day probationary period was over Marco was able to rent a modest apartment and move from his mother's home. After buying a truck only one month earlier it was a proud moment for him and a huge relief. No more bouncing back and forth between Nae's and his mom's home. Now he had a place he could call his own, even if it was empty as hell, containing little more than a bed with a box spring and a twenty-seven-inch television. He was starting over and he knew everything would take time.

To celebrate was the plan tonight, but it was more than just a celebration of him gaining his independence back. Tonight was a big night in a lot of different ways. It was his friend's Kevin birthday, and Kevin had decided to throw a party at a big hall and invite all of his coworkers. Marco knew Farrah would be there. They had been discussing the party all week and she seemed to be genuinely excited to be getting out of the house for a change, but that wasn't the best part either. Over the past month Marco had grown fonder of Farrah than he would have ever admitted to anyone, but himself. She influenced a lot of his decisions when it came to Nae and now things were becoming rocky between them because Marco was growing distant.

The more he got to know Farrah, she held his attention to the point he could hardly find the time to give Nae the attentions she needed. It put a major strain on things before they could work out all the kinks and now Marco could feel the tension building between them. He was still being the best father he could be, but as far as Nae was concerned his mind was somewhere else. Just last night he finally told her that he didn't want a relationship, and Nae teared up right in front of him calling Marco a user. From her viewpoint, he understood why she would feel that way. To Nae, it seemed he waited until he was on his feet to have a sudden change of heart, but that wasn't the case at all. The truth was, this woman with a family of her own at home had steamrolled her way into his heart and he knew it was more than just lust. He couldn't give Nae his all with so much of his mind concentrated on Farrah. He had to have her. He had to know what it felt like to be with her and to capture her heart the way she had stolen his.

Tonight could be his one and only chance. The opportunity was blatantly obvious to him. Farrah had informed Marco that her boyfriend would be out of town for the weekend of the party leaving her free to do as she pleased. Although she hadn't agreed to do anything outside of attending the party, he knew this was his chance. The stars were aligned in his favor this night and a burning desire was Marco's navigational system as he arrived at the party all alone.

Inside he quickly spotted Kevin sitting at the top end of an extended table that stretched half the length of the floor. The party was BYOB and all sorts of drinks covered the table from one end to the other. Marco recognized a lot his coworkers at the table and even a few friends he'd grown up with. He went to greet his old friends he hadn't seen in years. He gave Kevin a pound and wished him a happy birthday while passing him a bottle of Remy Martin; Kevin's favorite drink. Shortly after he spotted Farrah coming through the door with her sister wearing a tight fitting, spaghetti-strap, red dress with a low cut showing off her amazing figure. Her hair was braided in brown zillion braids that dangled past her shoulders and her black stilettos accentuated her calf muscles as she quick-stepped through the crowd. Marco stood mesmerized for a moment until he realized he was staring and looked away.

****

Farrah spotted Marco from across the room and gave him a quick smile, but he turned away before he could see it. He was looking sexy as hell in Cult of Individuality blue jeans and short sleeve shirt. His facial hair was trimmed into a perfect goatee and his brush waves were enough to make a woman seasick if they stared for too long. Farrah greeted her closest coworkers with hugs while she just threw a half-wave at others. Kevin was standing by the table making room for someone to sit when she strolled over to wish him a happy birthday.

"Hey birthday boy, happy birthday!" she said with a smile.

Kevin extended his arms for a hug and although Farrah wasn't the hugging type when it came to men at her job, she didn't want to be rude, so she met him with a brief hug.

"Thank you, baby," Kevin said as he shot Marco a quick glance.

Marco didn't read anything into it because he was busy with his own agenda. Farrah then strolled over to the area where Marco was still standing and talking with friends. She punched him slightly in the arm as a greeting.

"What's up friend?"

"What's up friend?" Marco returned as he glanced up and down taking her all in. "You looking like the baddest thing up in here."

"Boy please, don't start with your game," she giggled.

"It's not a game. It is not a game," he repeated with lust in his eyes.

Farrah introduced the sister that Marco had heard so much about but never met. She looked a lot like Farrah to him only shorter. After that, she decided they should find a good table before they were all gone as the hall started to quickly fill up.

"I'll be back," Farrah promised as her and Fatima darted off into the crowd.

A couple drinks later, Farrah was loose enough to get up and hit the dance floor, but she was hesitant because she didn't want to dance by herself. She was about to asked Fatima, but just then Kiara came through the door began her reign as the life of the party. As Trina's song Look Back at Me, blare through the club speakers as Kiara ran up on to the table where Farrah, Fatima, and some coworkers sat and broke out in a twerk dance, performing for anybody who was looking.

"Aaaaahhhh shit!" somebody yelled and all the girls at the table seemed to rise to their feet simultaneously and start dance and shaking ass everywhere. Farrah and Fatima danced on each other in between giggles as the alcohol they had consumed took over. A crowd formed around them as they made their own dance floor right in their section. Some of the dudes from the job joined them throwing hands in the air and singing the hook.

Farrah looked to her right and there was Marco vibing right along with the song hands in the air as well. Without a second thought, she danced her way over to him and before she knew she was backing her ass up on him bumping and grinding. Marco's dick got hard instantly, but he was too busy feeling good to notice. All of the women had found someone to dance and freak on and the party was now in full effect. Ladies dancing on each other made the room even hotter as Marco and Farrah just became lost in their own little world. The alcohol brought out the bad side to this good girl, and she showed no shame as she bent over to touch her toes while rubbing her ass back and forth on Marco's rod.

He was so tempted to try and take her right there on the floor as jealous men watched on from a distance in shock. Marco just could believe this was the same girl he had be getting to know for the better part of three months. There was no sign of this split personality before, but he was damn glad her alter ego had shown up tonight. If he didn't fuck her tonight his name wasn't Marco. After dancing two songs Farrah was tired and Marco was horny. As soon as he could Marco pulled Farrah into a corner.

"Why you playing with me like that girl?" He said invading her space as she sipped her on third and final drink. By now Marco was tipsy too and he knew the clock was ticking on his time to make a move.

"I don't know what you talking about," she said blushing away.

"You know what I'm talking about. Backing that big ole ass up on me like I don't know what to do with it."

"I ain't say nothing like that," she responded but her eyes told the truth.

"Well, you really ain't gotta say it, cause I'm saying it," Marco whispered as he moved in even closer. He glanced up and saw Kevin watching him from afar. By now it was no secret to anyone at work that to two of them were too close to be just coworkers, but no one said anything.

"What are you trying to say to me, Marco?" Farrah flirted.

"Shit, I ain't gotta spell it out, you know what it is. I want you bad as hell. I been nice and I been patient, but tonight I want that pussy. I deserve that pussy."

Farrah burst into laughter as she became extremely turned on by his aggressiveness. Her wild side had brought out Marco's animal instincts to hunt his prey and capture as if she was his next meal.

"I don't even know what to say right now," Farrah admitted as it all came to a head like she knew it eventually would.

"Say yes. Say you gonna dip out this party with me right now. Did you drive?"

"No...I um... I rode with my sister," she said truthfully as she contemplated Marco's offer.

"Good let's get out of here while it's still kinda early. We can follow your sister home and make sure she good if you want."

A Doughboys Cashout song came on and Kiara's loud mouth could be heard rapping over the music.

/Riding with a bad bitch you ain't never seen before/

/My baby mama know her name but she ain't never seen her doe/

Everyone seemed to be in a zone having a great time as the party erupted, except for Kevin. Kevin was still watching Farrah and Marco from afar.

"Let me see if my sister ready to go yet," Farrah finally decided.

Marco played it cool, but he was dancing on the inside.

"I'll be right here."

****

Farrah talked things over with her sister and they left the party shortly after. Marco and Farrah followed Fatimah to the freeway and after that, they went their separate way. As they rode in Marco's truck Farrah was thinking she was glad her sister wasn't judging her. It made things so much easier to know that she wasn't being frowned upon. Farrah was having more fun than she could remember having in years and she didn't want the night to end. She enjoyed every minute she spent with Marco and her desire had been building right along with his. By now her pussy was throbbing at the thought of what could happen next. The freak in Farrah was more alive than ever as they moved swiftly through traffic. Marco couldn't get home fast enough as he could feel her eyeballing him like a piece of meat.

"So I guess I'm about to meet the little fella huh? Farrah blurted out teasing Marco.

"Li'l fella? You ain't bout to meet know li'l fella tonight. You about to meet Mr. Bullhead," he shot back sending Farrah into a fit of laughter.

All of sudden she reached over and unzipped his jeans.

"Let me see," she mumbled with a sly grin.

Marco didn't refuse, but he found it hard to concentrate on the road with Farrah's hand fondling his rock hard penis.

"Mmmmmm," she moaned as if the feel of his rod gave her pleasure. "You not gonna judge me right?" she asked.

"What? Why would you even think that? This ain't just about fucking. You actually mean something to me," Marco finally admitted in the heat of passion.

After hearing him say that, Farrah let go of all of her inhibitions. She was ready to give him her body because he already had a piece of her heart. Farrah slid Marco's rod out of his jeans then leaned over the console and took him inside her warm and cozy mouth. The sensation of her touch was incredible and almost too much to bear and still handle the wheel. Marco found himself letting his head fall back more than once. By the way, she bobbed so bravely up and down on his pole Marco knew at that moment, Farrah was a real freak.

"Goddamn girl," he heard himself say. He had something in store for her. He was gonna show her ass tonight.

As soon as Marco turned his keys in the door he pulled Farrah inside and grabbed two hands full her butter soft booty and begin to nibble away at her neck. The softness of her skin made him eager and on fire inside. With his rock hard body press against her softness, Farrah grew moist as she stood by the door letting Marco have his way with her. He slid one hand up her dress and rubbed between her heated thighs. He could tell Farrah was more than ready. He grabbed her by the hand and led the way into the bedroom, but when they reached the threshold he stopped and slapped her on the ass.

"Get yo ass in that bed, I'll be right back," he ordered.

Farrah's eyes grew big as a grin spread across her face.

"Okay daddy," she shot back and did as she was told.

Marco went to the kitchen and grabbed the fruit bowl he had previously prepared right before he attended the party. It was finally about to go down. When Marco made it back to the room Farrah had slipped out of her heels and dress and was lying in his bed playing with herself. At that moment he wanted to give God a shout out but didn't think the Lord would approve. He stood for a second admiring all of the heavenly body that laid before him as Farrah continued to play inside of her panties.

"What's in that bowl?" she finally asked.

"Oh, you about to find out."

"Uh oh," Farrah cooed as she quickly realized what she was in store for.

Marco tore off his clothes and tossed them on the floor as he climbed in bed with Farrah and attacked her like a hungry dog gnawing at her neck and chest. He kissed her with a passion meant for only someone you loved and she returned his passion. His tongue began to explore her entire body. He kissed her from her chin to her toes. He held one foot in his hand, as he nibbled at her toes like a chicken dinner before he worked his way back up to her thighs. He sucked on her inner thighs before taking his first taste of her dripping wet pussy. He finally slid her panties off and kneeled down on both knees. With both hands cuffing her voluptuous booty he lapped softly at her kitten, exploring it. Farrah moaned lightly enjoying his gentleness. His tongue circled pussy lips and then plunged deeper inside of her than any tongue ever had. Again.

"Mmmmm," she moaned as her back arched.

"Yeah, I know," he whispered as he continued.

Marco sucked on her lips and flicked his tongue at her click until Farrah began to shout out to the man above. Then he rose up and grabbed the fruit bowl containing sliced peaches and grapes. He sat the bowl in the bed as Farrah watched on, burning with curiosity and anticipation. He took some grapes into his hand and massaged her clit with them. He then slid a grape inside her and used his tongue to retrieve it. Again. He repeated this seductive meal until only a few grapes remained in the bowl. He took the sliced peach into his hand and then slid inside of her. The smooth curve of sweet fruit felt like a moistened tongue teasing at the tip of her wetness. Just as he did with the grapes Marco retrieved the peaches with his tongue lapping up the syrup juice along with all of Farrah's body fluids until she just couldn't take anymore. She grabbed him by the back of the head as his lips clamped down on her clit and she squirted cum all in his face. Marco sucked it up enjoying every minute of it.

"Oh shit! Fuck me... fuck me right now," Farrah begged as soon as she caught her breath.

"As you wish," Marco said wiping his mouth as Farrah handed him the condom he had lain out on top of the nightstand. Farrah was still holding one leg diagonally up in the air as he entered her from a missionary position. As soon he entered her love box, he felt a sense of validation. Being inside her felt like the closest thing to heaven he could ever feel. As Marco gave her long gentle strokes he questioned whether the condoms was still on his dick or had it magically disappeared. Her goodness felt better than any pussy he'd ever raw dogged. His dick was so rocked he felt like it was growing inside her. As he plunged deeper and deeper Farrah shrieked with pain and pleasure.

"Oh God!" she cried.

He pulled out just as it was getting too good to him. He had to take his time and make sure he went the distance. If this was a one-time deal he had to put down right. He lay on his back.

"Come ride this dick for me," he commanded.

Farrah pushed herself up from the bed already a little woozy from intercourse.

"Anything you say, daddy."

As Farrah mounted him she could feel his pole slowly filling up her insides. She arched her back as sensations tickled her entire body. She balanced herself with both hands on his bulging pecks, gyrating her hips slowly until she was sure she could handle all of it. Once she found a rhythm she put some back into. Marco palmed one ass cheek and slapped the other. Every pump, thrust, and motion was in unison and it just felt like the two of them grew deeper in sync with every collision. Farrah fucked him rodeo style until she ran out of gas. She then bent down all fours as Marco plunged in from her backside. He wrapped his hands around her slim waist and took command of the pussy. The sound of hot, sweaty bodies slapping together could be heard echoing through his apartment, along with the screams, huffing and panting of two animalistic lovers. Marco could feel

Farrah's body tense up as her legs began to shake right before he exploded inside of the condom like never before. Farrah had already cum twice as she collapsed beside him breathing heavily.

For a while neither one of them said anything. They just laid there enjoying the bliss of the moment and developing their own individual thoughts about what had just happened.

"That was good," Farrah finally said.

Chapter 9

After taking a long breather, Farrah climbed on top of Marco, lying on his chest with her legs on the side of him. She planted a soft kiss on his lips.

"I should get up and get dress," she acknowledged.

"You don't have to. You could stay here and we could do a replay."

"Ha! As tempting as that sounds, I told my trusted babysitter I'd be home by 2:30 at the latest and it's already-"

All of sudden Farrah was interrupted by a loud pounding on Marco's front door.

"The fuck?" Marco said in total shock.

The first thing came to his mind was his parole. If police were knocking at his door that meant he was in some kind of trouble. He had been out all night violating all kinds of stipulations to his parole by drinking and driving and hanging out past his curfew. The pounding continued as he made his way to the door. His heart hammered on the inside of his chest like the banging going on outside his door. He peeked through the peephole trying not to be notice and spotted Nae standing outside his door with the meanest scowl. *Fuck is she doing here?*

"Why you banging on my door like you the fucking police?" he yelled through the door.

"What?" Nae said as her neck jerked back with even more attitude than she'd came with. "Why you talking through the door? Open the door."

"Why you come over here this late?" he questioned still not reaching for the door.

"Marco fuck you! You come to my house this late all the time. You must got a little bitch up in there, that's why you don't wanna open the door huh?"

Nae could be heard up and down the hallways. If was late and people were trying to sleep.

"Stop all that fucking yelling outside my door. How you get in here anyway?"

"Don't worry about it, is you gone open the door or not?"

Marco glanced back and saw that Farrah had appeared in the living room fully clothed with fear in her eyes. This wasn't what she wanted and Marco knew it. Farrah would hate to be put in a position where she had to defend herself. She wasn't a fighter and never pretended to be, but if she had to cut a bitch she would. As Marco and Nae went back and forth, Farrah threw her hands in the air emphatically as if she was asking for an explanation. Marco didn't have one.

"Nae go home, I'll call you in the morning okay?"

"Naw that's alright you don't gotta call. You call that bitch you with right now in the morning."

Boom! She kicked his door as she made her dramatic exit.

"Oh my God!" Farrah squealed wondering what in the world had she gotten herself into. "Take me home," she said shaking her head in disbelief.

"Okay... just give me a second so we don't run into her. Let me go get dress."

Marco rushed to the bedroom while Farrah chose to stay in the living room and pace the floor. If felt like some kind of bad karma had boomeranged on her minutes after her infidelity, leading her to believe she had just made a huge mistake. *What if she had just made an enemy for life?*

"Can we go now?" she pressured, thinking all kinds of crazy thoughts.

"Farrah, calm down. We good alright?"

"I don't wanna calm down, I wanna go home."

Marco was never a woman beater, but right now he felt like driving over to Nae's house and waiting in the bushes to punch her in the face when she arrived. She had just ruined one of the most magical night he'd had in recent history.

"Come on," Marco said as he appeared from the bedroom fully clothed.

Farrah told Marco to drop her off at her sister's house and after that, she didn't say another word. She didn't know if Marco was to blame or not. All she knew was she was frighten to the point she was shaking when Nae showed up and she hated that feeling. Nothing Marco could say would change the way she felt, but he tried anyway.

"Farrah, I'm truly sorry about that, I don't know what she was thinking showing up at my crib like that."

Farrah didn't respond. All she wanted was a hot shower and a warm bed. It was a good thing her man was out of town because with all the commotion she didn't even have time to wash the sex off her body. "You not gon' talk to me?" Marco continued.

"Ain't nothing to say. This was a mistake."

With that said, Marco left it alone and drove Farrah to her destination. As she exited the truck and pushed his passenger door shut, the closing clink of the door sounded so final. It reminded him of the door he had worked so diligently to get open and now it seemed to be locked all over again.

"Damn," he said aloud as he pulled from the curb.

As Marco drove home he tried his best to look at the bright side of thing. *He'd already gotten what he wanted, he tried to convince himself. If it was a one-time deal then so be it. Besides, she has a man and nothing last forever. It was fun anyway.*

Just when he was almost back home his cell phone rang and the caller ID read Mama. He rushed to answer knowing she wouldn't call this late if it wasn't important.

"Hello? Mama?"

"Yeah son," his mom answered with a quivering voice.

"Mama what's wrong?"

"It's your brother Trelly, son. Somebody shot Trelly tonight and he's dead. My oldest boy is dead," she cried out.

Marco couldn't believe his ears. The news hit like a ton of bricks to the chest as his foot slowly slipped off of the gas and he began cruising down Lasher doing ten miles per hour. He just rode and listened to his mother cry into the phone as he contemplated what could have happened to his one and only brother Trelly Well.

Chapter 10

Marco spent the night at his mom's house knowing she didn't need to be alone. She needed him there as a reminder that she still had one son left. From what police had been able to gather through their investigation, it seemed that Trelly had been shot and killed while attempting to break into someone's home. It was a hard pill to swallow for Marco knowing his brother went looking for trouble and found it in the worse way. At first, Marco plotted revenge on his brother's killer and even went so far as to make the call for a weapon the very next morning. But as he contemplated murder and what it meant for his young life, Marco began to realize that if someone had broken into his home and put him in that position, he would have reacted the same way.

It brought Marco no solace to know that revenge was not the answer. He was mourning his brother and feeling like he really needed someone to talk to when Nae and Mariah showed up at his mother's house early that afternoon. By then he'd realized that more than likely Nae had come to his apartment the night before to tell him about his brother. He felt like he owed her a huge apology.

"Hey Scoota," Marco said calling Mariah by the nickname he'd given her when she was a baby.

Mariah walked over and stood between his legs as he sat on the couch. Just seeing his daughter's face lifted his spirits a little. He picked her up and sat her on his lap then kissed her on the cheek. "You miss daddy?"

"Yeah."

"You ain't lying to me is you?"

"No."

"Good," Marco said with a smile.

"It was her idea to come," Nae said still bitter about last night. Her tone was nonchalant and her eyes rolled around in her head as if she was being held there against her will.

"Listen, I know you came by last night to tell me about Trelly and I'm sorry for the way I reacted. I wish you would've just told me what you were there for."

Nae didn't respond. It all honesty, she didn't find out about his brother's death until after she left Marco's apartment, but since he thought otherwise she decided it was best to keep it that way. In reality, she had shown up with intentions on ruining whatever plans Marco had for the night.

"How your mama doing?" she asked changing subjects.

"She's trying to be strong, but she hurting right now."

"I'm a go talk to her," Nae said as she pushed herself up on the sofa.

As Marco watched Nae exit the room a warm feeling came over his heart. She could be a sweetheart when she wanted to be. He knew at that moment he still cared for her even if she could be a jealous lunatic at times.

Nae and Mariah spent the entire day at Jeanine's house with Marco. Nae cooked dinner for everyone and tried her best to keep Marco and his mom in good spirits. For Marco, her presence was extremely welcomed at such a trying time. He had so much on his mind that he didn't want to think about, including all of the night before, so he gave Nae and Mariah his full attention. At the end of the night, Marco went home with Nae and they slept in the same bed but didn't have sex. Nae knew he needed her at a time like this and she was going to be his shoulder and show him what he would be giving up if he decided to give up on them being a family. She was now positive that she loved and wanted to be with Marco and it gave her great fear to think he didn't feel like they would be able to work things out.

For Marco, he was just trying to make it through the day. He wasn't dwelling on the future or the past at that moment. As he lay in bed next to Nae he continued to think about what he could have done differently to maybe help save his brother. He had already decided he was calling off from work in the morning because he knew he would be in no shape to show up and be productive. Nae just left him alone with his thoughts snuggling close to him in silence, but before she fell asleep she had to test the waters.

"I love you, Marco."

"I love you too Nae."

****

Monday morning Farrah went to work filling a little self-conscious about her and Marco being so blatantly obvious at the party Saturday night. After the baby mama drama, she thought herself a complete fool to let things go as far as they did. As she walked to her work stations she could feel the eyes following her, but she held her head up high. She was a grown woman and what she chose to do in her personal life didn't have a damn thing to do with these people, so they had better mind their business and keep their opinions to themselves. She dreaded walking past Marco's station and running into him, but to her surprise, he was nowhere to be found.

She figured he was probably running late, but as the day went on she began to search for him from a distance and he never showed up. She planned to keep away from him until he got the picture that whatever they had was short and sweet, but it was definitely over. Once he didn't show up she began to get a little worried. As much as they talked she felt like if he had planned to take the day off she would have known about it. His ongoing parole crossed her mind and her worried naturally intensified. By lunch time she got the news from Kiara who was told by Kevin that Marco's brother had been killed. The news saddened her and she didn't know how to move forward with the information. She felt as if she should say something, but didn't know if it was a good idea. After all, she was supposed to be weening herself off Marco and reaching out to him would only make things more difficult. At the end of the work day, she decided she could at the very least send him a text message to offer her condolences, so she did.

Farrah: Sorry for your loss. She text.

About ten minutes later she received a response from Marco.

Marco: I appreciate that. Can you call me, we really need to talk?

Dammit! This is exactly what I was afraid of, Farrah thought as she pulled away from the parking lot and headed to daycare. As she drove, she battled with her conflicting thoughts of curiosity and apprehension. She told herself she would make the call, but she would be firm and final if he wanted to discuss what happened Saturday. She hoped he didn't bring it up. She prayed he didn't, because she didn't want to be mean to him right now. He was suffering enough. She called him.

"Hello?" Marco answered in a sad tone.

"Hey."

"Hey. Thanks again for checking on me."

"No problem. You okay?"

"I'm getting there. My mom is taking it the hardest of course."

"I'll bet. I just wanted to check on and make sure you was okay, that's all," Farrah said in an attempt to make the conversation brief as possible.

"Listen, I don't really have a good explanation for what happened Saturday except the fact that I know Nae didn't come over there flipping out for no reason. She was actually there to tell me about my brother getting shot."

"Oh..."

Farrah didn't know how to respond to Marco's revelation so she just held the phone.

"I don't wanna lose you as a friend," Marco admitted.

"Well... we were friends before the sex became involved and I wish we would have just stayed that way. Now it's complicated."

"I don't think so. I mean, if you don't want that part of our friendship I'm not gonna try and force it. That don't mean things have to go back to hi and bye."

Farrah sighed.

"I don't know. I think right now the best thing for us is to just give each other some space."

"Okay. If that's what you want."

It wasn't at all what Farrah wanted, but she felt like it was what she needed.

"But at the same time, I know you going through a tough time so... I'm here if you need to talk," she found herself saying.

"That means a lot to me."

"You coming to work tomorrow?"

"Yeah, I'll be there."

"Okay. I'll see you tomorrow."

"Okay."

Farrah ended the call feeling just as confused as she did before she'd talked to him. It was so hard to be mad at him for things out his control, but she took the incident as a sign she was on the brink of causing some serious damage to her relationship. As she pulled up to the daycare all she could think about was Marco. It had been almost ten years since she'd gave her body to anyone other than Raheem. That fact that he'd fucked her like a champ with such a gentle touch didn't help her cause one bit. She knew it wouldn't be easy, but she had to shake Marco; get him out of her head and focus on home.

Chapter 11

In the coming days leading up the funeral, Nae was the perfect friend and companion to Marco. When he went to work he did everything he could to avoid Farrah, giving her the space she had asked for. After work, he would usually end up at Nae's house by the end of the night or vice versa. She would cook all his favorite meals, give him massages before bed, and oral pleasure followed by some of the best sex they had ever experience with one another. It felt like make up sex times ten. For the time being, Marco was completely over his infatuation with Farrah and he was slowly healing from the internal wounds his brother's death had inflicted upon him.

On the day of the funeral, Marco sat in the front row in a deeply squinted gazed, holding back tears, watching his brother's lifeless body as if he expected Trelly to wake up at any moment. His mother Jeanine sat to his left with Nae and Mariah on his right side holding hands. Jeanine sobbed in silence dabbing tissue at the corner of her eyes ever so often. She seemed to be holding up better than Marco expected. That was until his Aunt Marianne showed up and fell out in the aisle as soon as she spotted Trelly in a casket.

"Noooooo! Oh God nooooo! Noooooo!" Marianne screamed as his family members he hadn't seen in forever tried to pull her up from the floor. It was hard to tell if Marianne was genuinely consumed by her grief. Marco hadn't seen or heard from her in years, and he was sure his brother hadn't either. Whether her grief was authentic or not, it caused Jeanine to burst into an uncontrollable crying spell to the point she doubled over into his lap as her body jerked involuntarily.

"Mama, be strong for me okay? Be strong for me okay mama?" Marco begged as he tried to lift her upright and comfort her on his shoulder. It was tearing at his heartstrings to see his mother like this and he couldn't help but entertain the thought of revenge again. As soon his mom maintained her composure Marco stood then leaned over to Nae.

"Stay with her for a minute," he whispered right before he took off towards the exit.

Marco just couldn't take it anymore, so he went outside to get some air and gain control over his emotions that were running haywire at the present time. The ramblings of his mind felt like a toilet full of toxic waste as he paced outside the front door of the funeral home. His thoughts were interrupted by his friend Kevin approaching from the sidewalk.

"Hey, what's up man? Again, I'm sorry for your loss," Kevin said as he slapped fives with Marco and pulled him in for a tight-gripped hug. The two men conversed for a few minutes trying to take their minds off of what they were there for.

"Oh, I been meaning to tell you I need next Friday off. I gotta go in to see my P.O" Marco said.

"Okay, you know I got your back," Kevin assured him.

Since Marco wasn't a violent offender he was lucky enough that he didn't have to deal with the parole office that often. Once every two months he went in to show some pay stubs and drop urine then he was done with them. The brief exchange with Kevin was enough to divert Marco's attention from the malice that was flooding his mind and the two went inside.

****

That same afternoon Farrah sat at home feeling frustrated about the lack of attention she was getting from Raheem. For the first time, she began to realize she was unhappy with her current situation. Still very much in love with Raheem, Farrah felt she needed to be shown that he still felt the same way for her. Today she decided to be vocal about her feeling as she watched Raheem getting dress while she sat on the edge of their queen size bed.

"Where you think you bout to go?" Farrah asked.

"Where do I think I'm about to go? I know I'm about to go to my li'l cousin basketball game," Raheem assured her with confidence.

"Why didn't you ask me if I wanted to come?"

"Cause you don't watch basketball, Farrah."

"That don't mean I wouldn't go support your family," she countered.

The truth was she just didn't want to sit at home so it wouldn't matter where they went as long as they were together.

"Why would I drag you along if I know you only gonna be sitting there the whole time looking crazy and ready to go?"

"You don't know that. You know what? It don't even matter because the point is I'm tired of sitting at home by myself every weekend. It seems like all we do is go to bed together at night. We don't do shit, but work all week and then go our separate ways on the weekend. That's not a relationship."

As Raheem buttoned up his True Religion short sleeve shirt, he paused for a minute as she finished her vent. Farrah could see in his eyes that he was genuinely shocked by her words. Raheem hadn't given much thought to the way they had been living. It was just their routine, but once he realized she was unhappy, he immediately began to feel guilty. He took a seat next to her on the bed.

"I didn't realize that's how you felt about it. Why haven't you said anything before now?"

"It should be obvious. What woman doesn't want to be with her man?"

Raheem rubbed his hand across his face as he came to the realization of his neglectful attitude toward Farrah. She meant the world to him and he really couldn't imagine life without her. He was way too invested in their relationship to ever even think about losing her and having to start over. He knew he had to tighten up his game.

"I'm sorry if I made you feel less than wanted. You know what you mean to me. Don't you?"

"I used to," Farrah admitted.

"That's my fault. I know I been slipping, but I'm gon' tighten up."

"Is that a promise?" Farrah said as she gave him a skeptical glance.

"That's my word. Y'all wanna go to the game with me?"

"I don't know. Let me ask the boss man. Raheem!" Farrah yelled out calling her son into the bedroom and soon after Raheem Jr. came running as fast as he could.

"Huh, mama?"

"You wanna go to the basketball game with your daddy?"

"Yeah," Raheem Jr. said excitedly.

"Okay, go get your shoes," Farrah said.

****

The couple went to the game like a family and Farrah was content now. It felt good to know if she spoke up about a problem in their relationship she would be taking seriously. In hindsight, she realized that had she done it sooner maybe the whole Marco thing would have never happened. That thought sent her drifting back to the night they shared together. As Raheem came back from the concession stand with snacks she was lost in the thought of how good the dick was. His tongue game was just ridiculous. Raheem never ate her pussy like that. He hardly ever did at all.

"They didn't have fruit punch so I got you lemonade," Raheem said snapping Farrah out of her trance.

"Oh, thanks."

"You see little cuz out there fooling," Raheem said proud of his first cousin.

It was the first game of the new school year and Raheem had promised to make as many games as he could. Maybe this was something he could do with his family to show Farrah he didn't mind spending time with her. Farrah looked up and saw Raheem's cousin running up the floor and waving at them. She waved back, but Raheem didn't see him because he was playing with his son at the moment.

"He waving at you," Farrah said, but Raheem was enjoying the exchange with his son so much he didn't hear Farrah. "Marco...I mean, Raheem."

As soon as she uttered his name out loud she felt as if her esophagus was swelling. Raheem turned to her with the evilest scowl she'd ever seen.

"The fuck you just call me?"

Farrah's eyes widen as she searched quickly for words that escaped her grasp.

"I'm so sorry, I don't know where that came from," she finally said.

"You don't know where it came from? It came out your mouth, who the fuck is Marco?"

"Nobody, he's nobody. I was just thinking about something that happened the other day."

Farrah tried to brush it off, but Raheem was furious. The one thing she hated about him was the fact that he was insanely jealous. It brought out a whole other side of him.

"He must be somebody for you to look me in my face and call me another muthafucka name."

"I made a mistake, Raheem damn, I'm human," Farrah defended.

"We been together damn near ten years, have I ever called you another bitch name?"

"Another bitch? What's that's supposed to mean?"

"Another bitch, what you think it means?"

"Don't think you gon' disrespect me in public, I said I'm sorry."

Raheem was appalled at the idea that Farrah thought she could demand her respect after the disrespectful shit she had just pulled.

"Bitch, to get respect you gotta give it," he said getting all in her face.

The fact that he was doing this in front of a crowd of people was enough to make Farrah blow her top, but the fact that their son was sitting right there watching on was the thing that sent her over the edge. Farrah shot to her feet and stood over him as if she was seven feet tall.

"Call me another bitch in front of my son!" She shouted.

No one was paying them any attention until now. Now everyone around them was watching and wondering what was going on. Raheem couldn't believe what he was witnessing as he could not deny the fire in her eyes and the determination in her voice. She knew she couldn't win a fight, but right now she was willing to give a shot. As security looked on and began to head in their direction Raheem tried to keep a cool head.

"Farrah, you better sit the fuck down right now I swear," he growled through gritted teeth.

Farrah slowly calmed her nerves and sat back down. Only her love for her son would have made her react so aggressively. She knew she had made her point, but more importantly she had taken the heat off of the real issue momentarily. She was still in disbelief herself that she had called Raheem another man's name.

Chapter 12

"Sooooo guess who supposed to like me?" Kiara said to Marco as they worked side by side.

"Who?" Marco inquired.

"Your boy Kevin. I know he said something to you about me," she baited.

Marco was unaware of anything involving Kevin's personal life. They kept that part of their lives separated and Marco liked it that way. He didn't even know much about the girl Kevin had kids by or if they were still together or not. It wasn't his business.

"I ain't heard nothing," he explained.

"Liar. I know how y'all niggas talk. Anyway what' s up with you and your bitch?"

Marco was taking aback by the comment and the accusation. He hadn't made any claims of the sort.

"My bitch?" he questioned.

"Yeah, your bitch, y'all broke up or something?" Kiara said with a giggle.

"Just because you give me all your bullshit don't mean I'm gon' give you mind. I keep it G like I'm supposed to," Marco assured her.

"Mmmp. Alright then player," Kiara said with a grin.

Everyone had noticed the tension between Farrah and Marco at work. They went from seemingly best of friends to distance strangers overnight. It made for a lot of uncomfortable moments when they were around each other which was probably why Farrah seemed to avoid him as much as he did her. Marco had so much other stuff on his mind, he really didn't have time to dwell on it, but just as fate had lured them into each other's lives the universe could not suction enough gravity to keep them apart.

Trying to avoid the lunch room and more importantly Farrah, Marco had been going out for lunch most days on his break. Today was no exception, but he decided he was tired of eating burgers so he hit a Chinese takeout spot nearby. As soon as he stepped inside he spotted Farrah in line waiting to order. Out of all the places to go eat she had to pick here. He didn't even remember seeing her jeep in the parking lot. He felt foolish avoiding her and embarrassed every time she saw him and went the other way. As he looked around, he didn't see anyone else from work as he approached the counter behind her. He wanted to say something because while there was no bad blood between them, the lack of communication made it feel like there was.

"Farrah, what's up?" he spoke.

She had long ago noticed him but avoided eye contact until now.

"Hey, how you doing?" she spoke just to be cordial.

"I'm good. You know... I know we were supposed to be given each other space, but why it feel like we beefing? I'm not mad at you, are you mad at me?"

Farrah looked over her shoulder and up at him.

"No, I'm not mad at you, but you got me in trouble," she announced.

"Got you in trouble?" Marco said confused.

"Yeah."

"How?"

"Because, I called him Marco."

"Yo' nigga? Get the fuck outta here!" he chuckled.

"That shit ain't funny," Farrah said but had to laugh at her own stupidity.

"So what happened?"

"We had a big argument in front of a lot of people."

"May I take your order?" The cashier said interrupting.

As Farrah placed her order Marco took in the new revelation. No wonder she was running the other way every time she saw him. It all made perfect sense now. Maybe it was best they just went their separate ways, but as he stood behind her glancing down at her plump, salacious booty he couldn't help but feel conflicted, especially after having his way with her. Especially after knowing he had such a lasting effect. After placing her order Farrah turned to face him and see if he had anything else he wanted to say.

"Well, I'm sorry you got in trouble and hope you were able to patch things up fast. I don't wanna see you unhappy regardless of what happened in the past."

"We'll be okay, I guess," Farrah said referring to her and Raheem.

After the basketball game, they didn't talk the rest of the day. Eventually, Farrah convinced Raheem it was a simple slip of the tongue and he didn't bring it up again. The two continued to talk after Marco placed his order. It only made sense because the alternative was to stand there in silence while they waited. Neither one wanted to say anything that would lead toward dangerous topics. Farrah asked how he was dealing with his brother's death and he explained the best he could how he felt at the moment. When Farrah's food came she reached in her purse, but Marco stepped in front of her and placed a hand over hers.

"I got it," he said. "It's the least I can do for getting you in trouble."

Farrah completely agreed so she allowed him to pay. As she took in the sly grin on his face she couldn't help but admit she still enjoyed his presence the same as always. It felt good to be on speaking terms again, but that was far as she was willing to go.

"Thank you," she said giving him that smile he fell so hard for when they first met.

Damn he still wanted her ass.

After smashing a pepper steak dinner and a large Mountain Dew, Marco had to piss like a ninety- eight-year-old man with an unstable bladder. He rushed into the bathroom and overheard some fellas talking.

"It's been over a week now and Farrah still ain't fucking with that nigga," he heard Kevin say with a chuckle. As soon as Kevin looked up and saw Marco he froze like a deer in headlights.

"What's up doe?" Marco spoke playing it cool as if he didn't hear what he'd just heard. He felt like he was in a high school locker room instead of his job. He couldn't believe his friend was standing there talking shit and laughing behind his back. More importantly, he didn't understand why.

"What up, what up?" Kevin said as he quickly made his exit without ever looking Marco straight in the face. After Kevin left the other dudes in the bathroom followed suit.

"Niggas gossip just like bitches," he vented not caring who heard him.

When the work day was over Marco still could not stop thinking about Farrah. Her sexiness was so addicting that she infiltrated his thoughts constantly without warning. After the incident in the men's room Marco wanted her even more. Almost to give his new found haters-including his so-called friend something else to talk about. He knew there was some sort of jealousy involved, but Kevin was his boss so he brushed it off. As he sat at home flipping through channels Marco reflected on the conversation he'd had with Farrah in the restaurant. He chuckled again at the thought of her calling her man his name. Without even thinking about it, he grabbed his cell phone and scrolled through his contacts until he found Farrah's number under another name then he texted her.

Marco: *Sorry I fucked you so good you forgot your nigga name*

After a few minutes passed he received a text back.

Farrah: *Don't remind me I'm trying to forget.*

The two continued to text back and forth for the next twenty minutes. Marco explained he was trying to work things out with Nae, but admitted it was hard to let go of Farrah. Farrah agreed it was hard to let go and she missed having someone to confide in. Marco knew she still wanted his friendship even if she didn't want the extra benefits. Again, Nae became secondary as Marco developed his new strategy to possess Farrah.

Marco: *Maybe one day we can be friends again like we were*

Farrah never texted backed.

As the day winded down Marco plotted to win Farrah's heart once again. It consumed so much of his thought process he barely had time to dwell on his brother's death that had been eating at him so much. By the time he showed up at Nae's house he was half drunk and extra horny from the lust for Farrah building inside. He called her phone in the driveway.

"Hello?" Nae answered.

"Mariah sleep?"

"She better be, it's eleven o'clock. Why?"

"I'm outside, come open the door."

"K."

Marco chirped the alarm on his truck and climbed the steps two at a time. When Nae opened the door she was already wearing a bathrobe with a teddy underneath. He didn't know if it was the liquor he'd been drinking or what, but Nae was looking so good from head to toe at the moment he couldn't resist grabbing her by the robe and pulling her close to him. He cupped her ass and kissed her liked he hadn't seen her in months.

"How much you had to drink?" Nae said after their lips unlocked.

"Do it matter?" Marco answered with lust in his eyes.

He ran his hand up her long brown leg until he was able to stroke her pussy lips through her panties as he kissed on her collarbone and sucked on the exposed areas of her breasts.

"Mmmm," Nae exhaled deeply as her body temperature rose and her juices simmered.

Still standing in the middle of the living room floor Nae wondered would Marco have sense enough to take her to the bedroom in case Mariah woke up. He would not.

"Come on right here, right now," he said as he unbuttoned his Levi's.

Nae hadn't seen him come on to her this strong since he'd been home from jail and it made her feel extra sexy to know she still turned him on this way. She squatted to her knees and took hold of his thick black pole into her hand, stroking it gently. She took him inside her mouth and began to let her tongue do the honors. She wrapped her tongue around his shaft stroking it slowly with her lips in and out until she could feel his ultimate stiffness inside her mouth. She began bobbing up and down with porno tenacity until Marco pulled back. He grabbed her hand to help up from the floor then escorted her to the far end of her leather sectional.

"Bend that ass over," he demanded.

Nae obeyed the orders as her panties dropped to the floor and her robe flew open. Marco lifted her robe up and around her waist and plunged inside of her with one deep stroke.

"Mmmmm," Nae released as he pulled back then slowly slid inside her. He grinded his hips with slow, sneaky rhythm while trying to keep Nae from moaning loudly and waking Mariah. The slow grind was getting too good to keep it going and he eventually began to pound away at her backside. He grabbed Nae's hair as she tried her best to keep quiet, but with every thrust, she felt herself losing control. She bit down on her lip as he manhandled her pushing her head farther down into the lounge until she was pinned to a pillow. Marco exploded inside of her and continued to hump her backside like a dog in heat until he was all done. If Nae knew just how badly he needed that nut and why he was sure she would have stabbed him with something from the kitchen.

Chapter 13

As raindrops danced outside her window and lighting illuminated the dark room for a brief second at a time, Farrah lay stiff and wide-eyed staring into blackness. Her conflicting thoughts kept her from closing her eyes to rest. Ever since Farrah expressed her feelings to Raheem about them spending more time together he had stepped up his game. He was now making time for her every weekend. Sometimes it was something as simple as a movie date, but that was all she ever wanted anyway. But somehow, someway, Farrah still was feeling unsatisfied and daydreaming of Marco. Eventually, her daydreams turned to wet dreams and she would wake up feeling energized and refreshed as if her sexual encounters in her dreams were real.

As much as she wanted to keep her home life intact the allure of what she and Marco had started was becoming too much to fight. She knew that Marco wasn't going to let her go without a fight and it was that knowing that was slowly breaking down her mental resistance. *But why? Why was she so drawn to him?* That was the question that kept her unsettled and up half the night.

That morning Farrah woke up bright and early to make a big breakfast for everyone; pancakes, turkey bacon, scrambled eggs and grits. When Raheem woke up, he was surprised to see Farrah entering the room with a tall glass of orange juice and a big plate for him. She always cooked breakfast, but never served him in bed.

"Damn, foreal? What I do to deserve this?" Raheem asked.

"You listened to me," Farrah explained as she sat the plate on the nightstand and kissed him on the cheek.

"I been doing good, huh?" Raheem said with a big grin.

"Yeah," Farrah admitted as her guilty conscious scrambled her mind and kept her thinking of ways to please Raheem. "I think we should let him go over Fatima house today so we can chill," she said referring to her their son.

"Did you talk to her about that?"

"Yeah, I just got off the phone with her, she ain't got no plans."

"That's sounds like the move then. Where's he at anyway?"

"In the kitchen eating. He should be done by now, he probably in there playing around. Raheem Jr.!" Farrah called out to her son.

Seconds later he bent the corner faster than a speeding bullet, and once he saw his father was awake he dove straight in the bed ready to wrestle.

"Come on now boy, I'm about to eat back up."

Raheem Jr. wasn't hearing it. He tried to grab his father in a headlock but found his legs being swept out from under him, causing him to crash down on the bed in a fit of giggles.

"Stop playing and come here," Farrah commanded.

Raheem Jr. scooted to the edge of the bed.

"Huh, mama?"

"You wanna go over your Aunt Tima house today?"

"I wanna go over my Auntie Tima house!" he answered excitedly.

"That's what I just said."

"Unhuh, I wanna go."

"Alright, if you finished eating go get you some underwear so you can get in the tub."

Raheem Jr. jumped down off the bed and shot out of the room filled with delight, just knowing he was going to have loads of fun today. Farrah went inside her dresser drawer, dug down to the bottom and pulled out a pair of handcuffs. She tossed them on the bed in the most nonchalant manner as she headed out the room.

"Oh, you feeling like that, huh?" Raheem questioned, but Farrah didn't respond, she just glanced back at him and let her eyes convey the message.

****

Marco and Nae were chilling at Nae's house enjoying a nice quiet evening while Mariah was away with family. They had a feast for dinner that they'd bought from Crab House; grilled shrimp, tilapia and salmon salad. After stuffing their bellies, they sipped Hennessy and watched movies in the living room, caking like the old days. It felt good for the both of them to spend time together without all the beef and bickering. It made Marco think that maybe time would one day mature them both enough to give it a real shot. But even when the thought of having something real with Nae crossed his mind, the idea of letting go of his pursuit of Farrah seemed unfathomable.

Nae fondled and massaged his hand inside of hers as she intertwined their fingers and locked them gently.

"I love you," Nae whispered.

"I love you more," Marco professed, although it was more of what she wanted to hear and less of what he was sure he really felt. At the moment, Marco was about as decisive as a fat kid in a candy store being told to choose just one.

As if she was reading his thoughts Nae glanced at him.

"Do you really?" Nae ventured as she sipped her drink.

"I mean...yeah, why you say that?"

"I was just asking. I wanna believe that but...you know we been through a lot."

"That's only because you got a mean jealous streak," he chuckled.

Nae wasn't amused.

"No, that's because you done fucked a gang of bitches behind my back," she reminded him.

"Not a gang, maybe one or two. Three at the most," Marco said still laughing it off.

Nae punched his arm.

"That shit ain't funny!"

"Come on now, don't start tripping on the past, we having a good time tonight. Don't ruin it with your bullshit."

"You're right, I'm not gon' mention the past. The past is the past," Nae agreed, but still had a point that she wanted to reach. "I guess I just wanna make sure that I have you all to myself this time around."

"I understand."

There was a brief moment of silence.

"Soooo, do I?" Nae questioned.

"Come on Nae, I think we moving at a pretty good pace, we don't gotta rush into nothing."

"Okay, but we ain't just met yesterday. We have a five-year-old daughter together so what are we waiting on?"

"We ain't waiting on nothing, let's just let nature take its course."

Nae huffed.

"So let you fuck other bitches until you get tired?" she lashed.

"See, there you go with that dumb shit."

"Marco I'm not trying to start an argument, I just don't want my heart broke again, especially by you."

"I'm not gon' do that."

There was another brief pause when the alcohol began to distort Nae's thought process as she was bombarded with bad memories of lies and deceit. She needed to know Marco was serious before she let herself fall any deeper.

"So just answer me this, are you still seeing anybody other than me?"

"I'm not fucking nobody if that's what you asking me. Do I still have friends? Yes, because as far as I know, so do you."

"I don't have friends, especially the kind that I used to fuck. If you still have those type of friends, it just a matter of time before y'all fucking again."

"Come on now, you make it sound like I just got bitches tucked away all around the city when it ain't shit like that."

"So how many is it?" she pried. "How many of these so-called friends you got?"

"Why does it matter?" Marco said growing more frustrated by the minute.

"Because it matters, how many?" she pressured.

Marco was tired of going back and forth and didn't have the energy to make up shit.

"If you really want to know, it's only one person," he said honestly.

"Why?"

"Why, what? What do you mean, why?"

"Why is there one other person? Why can't it just be you and me?"

"I didn't say it couldn't be, but we not there yet. I mean, you make it sound like this was our plan. This wasn't our plan at all. We didn't have no intentions of getting back together when I came home but then shit started happening. That's why I keep saying let's just let things run its course."

"Whatever, it doesn't matter. Either we gon' be together or we not, simple as that."

Silence...

"Do you care for her?" Nae continued.

"What do you want from me, Nae?"

"The truth."

"Do I care for her? Yes, of course, I care about all my friends, that's why they're called friends. It's not like what you're thinking."

Before he could finish explaining his last statement, Nae was on her feet breathing fire as she stood over him removing the glass of cognac from his hand.

"Get out my house," she demanded.

"What? Girl I'm sitting up here tryna tell you something, it ain't even like that."

"I don't care what it is like, get out my house!"

"Man, you better chill out we supposed to be having a good..."

"I don't care, go over there with her and have a good time."

She pulled on his arm trying to lift him up.

"If I wanted to be somewhere else I would be, but I'm here with you."

"Okay, well, go over there with her."

Marco stood up angry now.

"You get on my fucking nerves!"

"I don't care! Go over there with her! Go over there with her! Go over there with her!" she continued to yell at an unreasonable volume.

Marco finally got fed up with all the yelling and snatched Nae in his arms.

"Shut the fuck up! I ain't come over here for all that," he scolded right before he wrapped her tightly in his arms so that she couldn't fight and began kissing down her neck.

"Let me go!" Nae cried, but her cries went on deaf ears.

"I ain't letting shit go," he mumbled holding her firmly in his clutches as he kissed the back of her ear knowing it was the spot that made her weak.

"Stop," she managed weakly.

"Shut up," he continued.

Marco slipped his tongue inside her mouth to keep her quiet and she kissed him back while the rest of her body struggled to break free from his grip.

"Let me go, Marco," she begged when she came up for air, but this time her words had no force behind them. His hold on her was a turn on now and she didn't want him to leave.

"I'm a let you go alright?"

Marco forced their bodies backward and onto the couch. He lay her down and climbed on top of her all in the same motion as he kissed in between her breast and worked his way up until their lips locked again. Now Nae was pinned down underneath him with nowhere to go. Their passion was too strong to fight so she just closed her eyes and gave in.

Chapter 14

Things were running about as smoothly as could be expected for Farrah and Raheem. She continued her friendship with Marco but was still trying with all her might to keep it platonic. Outside of her physical attraction to him, she really did enjoy the bond they had created as friends. Marco could peep the vibe so he just continued to be whatever she needed him to be for the moment without any pressure. He realized that if Farrah wanted him she would make it known and pressure from him could only have the opposite effect. He knew her now and he knew how to maintain and strengthen the connection he had already built. In Marco's mind, it was almost impossible that she wouldn't eventually succumb to her suppressed desires.

Meanwhile, Nae was happy to feel like she had finally gotten Marco to commit to a real relationship. It wasn't hard for Marco to realize it would make his life so much easier if he just told Nae whatever the hell she wanted to hear. Back at work Marco and Farrah were up to their usual routines. In the break room, Farrah was busy uploading some of the professional family portraits she had taken with her son and boyfriend recently. She glanced out of the corner of her eye and could see Marco approaching, peering over her shoulder at her phone.

"You so nosy," she giggled as she cuffed her phone pressing it lightly against her chest.

"I just seen you on a picture so I zoomed in for a closer look, that's all."

Farrah pointed her finger at her face as if to say he could just see her in person instead. Marco slapped her finger down and took a seat next to her.

"Punk!" she complained, punching his arm.

"You missed me?" he inquired.

"You missed me?" she countered.

"I asked you first."

Farrah made a small gap between her index finger and thumb.

"This much."

"Damn, that's all?"

"Boy shut up, that's a lot."

"You don't even call a nigga no more."

"I called you last week," she reminded him.

"Exactly."

Just then Marco's phone rang and it was Nae. She rarely called him at work because she was usually at work also and they didn't share the same lunch hour. He thought maybe something was wrong with Mariah so he answered quickly.

"Hello?"

"Hey bae," Nae said.

"Hey...something wrong?"

"Why something gotta be wrong?"

"Well for one, you usually working around this time, and two, you don't never really call me at work."

"We had a power outage at my job so they sent everybody home early. So I was just sitting here thinking about you and I wanted to call and say thank you."

"Thank me for what?" Marco asked confused.

"Well, you since you been home and we been working things out, I feel like I'm in a happy place again. Mariah is happy, and you kept your word on coming home and being a father to your daughter, so I just wanted to call and say thank you."

The gesture took Marco by complete surprise and made Marco feel a little emotional inside.

"I know you gon' be trying to rip my head off later on, but thanks, I really appreciate you saying that."

"No I'm not, long as you don't give me a reason," Nae said giggling.

By now Farrah had figured out that Marco was probably talking to Nae so she began scrolling her Instagram page and pretend not to be eavesdropping. As the conversation continued a hint of jealousy began to invade her thoughts. This was supposed to be her alone time with him, why couldn't they do that shit on their own time? She was tempted to call Raheem just because, but she knew he was busy working.

"So we ain't seen you in two days, you coming over tonight?" Nae questioned.

"Yeah, what you cooking?"

"I didn't take nothing out yet. What you want?"

"You know what I like, surprise me."

"Alright, well, be good at work, and I'll see you later.'

"Alright, see you later."

"Love you."

"You too," Marco mumbled in returned without saying the actual words.

For some strange, stupid ass reason, he wasn't comfortable telling his girlfriend he loved her in front of Farrah. When he ended the conversation Farrah was typing a comment under her photo on Instagram. He could tell she was listening by how hard she was trying to pretend that she wasn't. When she was done she showed Marco the picture he was trying to see earlier of her and her family. She only showed him the photo because of the petty jealousy she was feeling at the time. She wanted to remind him that she had someone in her life that loved her too.

"Ain't y'all cute, rocking the same colors and shit?"

Seeing Farrah with her family was a little bit of reality check for Marco. Knowing it and seeing it was two different things. She really did have a whole life that was created long before him and had nothing to do with him, but then again so did he. It was all kind of crazy, but none of it would detour him from getting what he wanted which was Farrah. As she went into detail about the day of the photo shoot, Marco sat listening and admiring her beauty in awe. Her hair was different. She had a spiral wet look that made her look so exotic. Damn she was fine. He had to have her...he just had to.

Once Marco came out of his trance of fantasizing, he looked up and spotted Kevin in the corner eating and watching them. It was odd to see him in the lunch room. Marco couldn't remember seeing him ever eating in the lunch room the entire time he'd been there. Once they made eye contact Kevin turned and pretended to be involved in a conversation that was going on at his table without him. Since the day Marco overheard Kevin and his other co-workers gossiping in the bathroom about he and Farrah, their relationship had changed drastically. They hardly ever spoke two words to each other unless it was work related. A few minutes passed and Marco noticed for the second time Kevin discreetly leering from afar.

For the first time, Marco realized there had to be a hint of jealousy lingering in Kevin's heart. His actions revealed his true feelings. He could tell a lot of his coworkers held contempt for him because of Farrah, but he was disappointed in Kevin because they were supposed to be friends.

****

A few days passed after the strange behavior from Kevin, but soon after Marco was hit with a monkey wrench upside his whole program. Kevin came to him and informed him that the second shift was behind in their work and they needed some of the first shift workers to step in and help out. Marco would be transferred to second shift, effective immediately. This was a major setback as he wouldn't see Farrah at all just as he was laying his new foundation and reestablishing her trust. Pissed couldn't begin to describe his feelings.

He hated second shift from the very first day. He didn't know anybody and all the supervisors seemed to be on edge about things falling behind on their shift. The tension was high and the work was harder, but he pushed through it hoping the time would pass quickly.

Although the transfer was mandatory for some people, Marco questioned the motivation behind Kevin's decision when he was chosen for second shift. The chosen few were supposedly those with the least seniority, but Marco knew for a fact he had seniority over at least three guys who were not chosen and had started the job after him. He hated entertaining the idea that his childhood friend had it out for him, but the more he mulled it over it was certainly starting to feel that way.

Chapter 15

The past two weeks without Marco around had given Farrah a bad case of the lonelies. She missed him dearly and to make matters worse it seemed Raheem was slipping back into his same old ways again. They were back to going their separate ways on the weekends with a little pit stop for sex. *Why couldn't Raheem get it through his head that life was more than going to work and fucking? Was it so hard to date a woman once he had her? Was it so hard to spend time and converse with her like they used to? Maybe if he gave her the time and attention she deserved another man wouldn't be able to come along and gain her attention so easily, she thought.*

Every day that she sat in the break room making small talk with her female coworkers it was a constant reminder that Marco was not around. Although they talked on the phone when they could, it was hard for both of them to get free time now with him working on a different shift. She hadn't seen him at all except for the one time he just happened to be pulling in the parking lot just as she was leaving. Today she sat in the break room all alone chowing down on some chicken nuggets and was surprised when Kevin popped up at her table and invited himself to a seat right across from her.

"What's up Farrah," he spoke.

"Hey," Farrah waved feeling awkward.

Kevin was cool, but they hardly ever conversed outside of work related things. It was usually just hellos and goodbyes.

"You enjoying lunch," Kevin asked starting his attempt at making small talk.

"It's alright," Farrah responded. "Where's yours at?"

"I had a big breakfast so I decided to skip lunch."

"Mmpt."

Kevin scanned the room as Farrah continued to eat, feeling more awkward by the second.

"Hey listen, why don't you take my number down and give me a call sometime. I know you got a boyfriend and everything, but I really wanna get to know you better," Kevin confessed.

Farrah couldn't believe what she was hearing. She knew Kevin had a little thing for her, but she had already shut him down politely long ago. She couldn't believe he would try this now, knowing her relationship with Marco.

"You know I can't do that," she said with a polite smile.

"Why not?" Kevin persisted.

"You know why."

"No, really I don't. Can you explain it to me?"

Farrah knew Kevin was fishing at that point. He wanted her to openly admit that she was seeing Marco after shooting him down, sighting her boyfriend as the reason. It was a bitch move and Farrah was losing more respect for Kevin as he continued to talk.

"What's understood don't need to be explained," she finally said.

"Oh yeah?" Kevin said with a raised eyebrow. "Okay then, enjoy your lunch break," he finished as he stood to leave.

"You too."

Some friend, Farrah thought as she watched Kevin exit the room. *What did he think she was some type of whore that would just fuck whoever was around at the time?* To Farrah, her friendship with Marco was about so much more than sex. As a matter of fact, sex was probably the least important factor of it. She was sure no other man could take his place and she damn sure wasn't taking any applications. She hadn't reached out to him in over a week, but she was certainly going to let him know about the stunt Kevin tried to pull.

When Farrah got home, she got her son settled and then called Raheem to see just how long he would be out without asking him outright. Once she realized he wouldn't be coming straight home from work, she took the time to reach out to Marco while she had a chance. Going by her own schedule she was able to calculate what time his first break would be and she texted him.

Farrah: You on break?

Marco: Yeah

Farrah: Can I call you real quick?

Marco: Of course

Farrah called Marco and when he answered she could hear the jubilation in his voice, exposing how happy he was to hear from her. The feeling was mutual and the two went on to talk over each other repeatedly they were so excited. They both had so much to say that they couldn't possibly get it out all in time over a fifteen-minute break. As she glanced at her watch

Farrah didn't want the conversation to end. She missed him so much and she hadn't even had a chance to tell him about Kevin yet.

"I wish the break was longer," she admitted.

"Me too, I feel like I'm on a call from jail or something waiting for the operator to say my time is up."

"I'll try to call you again when I get a chance."

"Farrah, I really wanna see you. I miss you and I can tell you miss me too."

"Of course I do but..."

Space and time had shortened Marco's patience and increased his desire.

"Come on Farrah, don't give me no but's, just tell me you'll come see me this weekend."

"You gon' try to get me naked," she accused.

"Not if you don't want me to."

"Whatever."

"Is that a yes?"

Farrah was caught up in a tailspin of emotions. She was dying to see him but knew where it would lead to. It was becoming too much of a challenge to keep pushing Marco away and too hard to keep denying her feelings.

"My break is over so I gotta go. Can I expect to see you or am I playing myself right now?" Marco asked one last time.

Farrah sighed once she made her decision.

"If I'm free this weekend, I'll come and see you, Marco."

"Okay, I'll take that as a yes. Call me when you can."

"Okay, bye."

When Farrah ended the call she heard a noise coming from her bedroom. Raheem had come in without her even realizing it. Her heart skipped a beat and then began to pound at a rapid pace as she grew frightened he'd overheard her conversation. She slowly eased from the kitchen to the bedroom where Raheem was removing the clip from his pistol. She was about to ask how he ended up home so fast, but seeing the gun froze Farrah in her tracks. Raheem had a gun permit, but never carried his gun. It was usually locked away safely.

"You carried your gun today?"

"Yeah," Raheem answered as he locked the gun away."

"Why?"

"Shit, you ain't been watching the news? These niggas out here carjacking like crazy."

Farrah exhaled deeply after realizing she hadn't been overheard at all, but the close call was a vivid reminder of the fact that she was playing with fire, and that could be dangerous.

****

The days leading up to the weekend rendezvous, Farrah and Marco talked or texted every day. It seemed like the distance between them had brought them closer together. Farrah thought it over and concluded she was no longer going to push Marco away. Despite her apprehension, she was now inviting him to come closer; closer to her mind, body and heart. Raheem was not giving her what she needed. She went all in, cards on the table, face up, so did Marco. Once again, Nae took a back seat to Farrah as Marco's thoughts became predominantly about her.

The day Farrah agreed to come over Marco was up bright and early preparing his home for her presence. He cleaned the place from top to bottom, vacuuming the carpet, sweeping and mopping all the floors. He did seven hundred pushups so he'd looked extra buffed when she arrived. He broke out his favorite cologne and some of his best gear from the closet. He decided to go with a Polo short set and some matching Polo boat shoes. As he peeked in the mirror brushing his waves over and over, he wondered why he never went through so much trouble for a visit with Nae. He still had real feelings for Nae, but she didn't bring out the will to go the extra mile the way Farrah did.

An hour before she was set to arrive, he made a run to the liquor store to get some drinks. He told Nae he had to handle some business for his mom and he'd be tied up until later. Around seven o'clock his phone rang and he knew it was Farrah before he answered the phone.

"What's up?" he answered.

"What's upper?"

"I'm just sitting here counting down the minutes."

"Lies."

"If you know me, you know it's true."

"Mmm hmm."

"Where you at?"

"About ten minutes away from you."

"Oh okay, well get your fine ass over here," he demanded.

"Yes daddy," Farrah responded encouraging his aggressiveness.

When Farrah pulled up into the parking lot of Marco's building she felt butterflies fluttering around in her stomach, making her feel like a school girl again. She couldn't remember the last time Raheem gave her butterflies, but it was becoming routine with Marco. Dress in a long sundress and sandals, she flounced to the entrance. Marco buzzed her in and on the elevator ride up she felt those butterflies again, but this time she contributed it to the elevator. When Farrah arrived at Marco's door it was slightly ajar so she fingered it open and eased inside. Marco was pouring himself a stiff shot of Redberry Ciroc over ice. He looked so heavenly and chocolate as he swaggered towards her with his arms stretched wide to embrace her. Marco took her into his grip lifting her completely off her feet as his cologne engaged her senses. It felt so good to be in his arms again.

As he held her suspended in midair and looked into her eyes, Farrah tilted her head downward and kissed his lips. Once again they entered a world of their own making, where no one else was invited.

"I guess you really did miss me huh?" Farrah said as she was finally released.

"You better know it."

As she fell into the sofa, Farrah slid off her sandals and got comfortable. Marco poured her a drink and brought it to her. She sipped.

"Mmm, that's good."

"It's not too strong?"

"No it's perfect," she assured him with a thumbs up.

"Cool. So how's home life," Marco asked taking a seat next to her.

"We got into a big argument yesterday."

"You and your dude?"

"Yeah."

"About what?"

"Because, this nigga just left his gun out on the nightstand while he went to the bathroom. I was like, is you crazy muthafucka?"

"He carry a gun?" Marco inquired with a raised eyebrow."

"Yeah, he just started carrying it recently because of all the carjacking and stuff. But I cussed his ass out big time, he know I don't play about no guns around my son. I don't care if the door was close."

"I feel you. I actually just got a new pistol myself when I heard some people in the building had their apartments broken into."

"You can't get a gun license, you're a convicted felon," Farrah reminded him.

"That won't stop me from blasting a nigga if I catch him in my shit."

"I don't like guns," Farrah complained as she took a sip of her drink and stood up to venture around Marco's apartment.

"What you looking for nosey?"

"You can tell a lot about a man from his home."

Farrah was impressed at how clean his place was the few times she had visited him. She peeked in the bathroom then tipped toed toward the bedroom for a peek. She didn't even hear Marco creep up behind her. He wrapped his arms around her waist.

"You go in there, you might not come out for a while," he whispered in her ear before planting a kiss on the back of her neck. She could feel the bulge in his pants pressed against her booty.

"Really?"

"Yeah, you wanna go in there?"

"Nope," she responded, breaking his grip and heading back to the living room. She sat back down on the sofa and continued sipping her drink. Marco downed his glass of Ciroc and set it on the coffee table. He then got down on both knees, right in front of Farrah. He began to massage her thighs gently.

"I just wanna taste it," he confessed.

"What?" Farrah giggled.

"I just wanna taste that sweet shit."

He slid both his hands up Farrah's sundress. She didn't resist.

"Oh God," she mumbled knowing he really about to put the moves on her.

111

She took a big gulp from her glass of Ciroc as his hands eased up her thighs and finally reached her thongs then slid them off. She stepped out of her thong and closed her eyes as Marco's head disappeared underneath her dress. Moments later, she was firmly reminded of why Marco had become such an addiction. It was like her pussy and his tongue were the best of friends. Never in her life had a man been able to handle her with such care; such detail that chills ran up her spine with his every move. If he kept this up it wouldn't be long before she'd be begging for his dick inside of her. Her body shuddered as her head flew back and her mouth fell open, but no words came out; just short gasps for air. She couldn't take it anymore.

"Okay, okay. You win!" she announced.

When Marco came up for air Farrah stood up and shot straight to his bedroom coming out of her sundress with each step until it dropped to the floor. Marco followed closely behind watching her ass jiggle all the way. He felt like a jungle warrior hunting his prey as he grabbed his pole bulging out of his shorts. Marco sat on the bed and quickly stripped. Farrah came around in front of him and pushed him back on to the bed. She grabbed his rod and guided it into her mouth without hesitation. As she bobbed her head up and down Marco was amazed at how she devoured his shaft with such remarkable technique, even licking his balls. At that moment he really couldn't see a chance in hell that he would ever let her go. She filled his every need sexually. She forced moans from his mouth as he tried to contain himself. The pleasure he felt was almost unbearable.

"Goddamn girl!" he finally caved.

Just then Farrah came up smiling shyly. She was every man's desire; a lady in the street, but a freak in the bed.

"I got yo' ass, you gon' learn today muthafucka," Marco assured her as he lay her down and reached for the condom in his nightstand only to find the space was empty.

Just then he remembered using the last condom the last time he'd had sex with her. This couldn't be happening. As he lay stretched across the bed clueless on what to do now Farrah fingered herself keeping her pussy hot and ready.

"Unfucking believable!" he finally said.

"What's wrong?" Farrah said as her fingers paused.

"I thought I had a condom in here, but I don't."

"Are you serious?" Farrah roared.

"I wish I wasn't."

Farrah was beyond pissed and it was all over her face.

"I can't believe this shit!" she vented.

Farrah was horny and irritated to the max. Marco quickly wrapped his arms around her and began planting kisses everywhere.

"Don't be mad at me. We can still make this work."

"How?"

"We can do it just this one time without one," he suggested still kissing all over her body.

"No, we can't."

He licked her neck and nibbled on her collarbone as the taste of her skin settled his growing frustration.

"Just this one time," he pleaded as his hands ventured from around her waist and in between her thighs. Farrah was so confused and horny it was hard to focus. More than anything she wanted him right now. She knew Marco wasn't the type to be philandering through the city, but what he was asking was a hug bet on trust.

"I don't know Marco," she said as he began to suck her nipples and she tried to make a decision on whether to stop him now or let him continue to arouse her. It felt so good as his hands and lips explored her entire body.

"I promise I won't ask again, just this one time," he whispered.

"Are you one thousand percent sure you're safe?"

He lifted his head and looked in her eyes.

"I'd die before I let anything happen to you. Yes I'm sure."

Farrah didn't say anything else and neither did Marco. She closed her eyes and let him continue to have his way with her. When he dug into her juice box raw it felt even more sensational than the first time for the both of them, but with every stroke Farrah fell deeper in love.

Chapter 16

Farrah lay in Marco's arms enjoying the euphoria and recovering from the physically draining experience they'd just shared. After a few more minutes she forced herself up from the bed and went to find her cell phone.

"Can you get me a wash cloth and a drying towel?" she called out to Marco who was still savoring the moment, lost in thought.

He didn't want to move from the bed, but he had to get up and change the cum stained sheets and clean himself up as well.

"Oh shit!" Farrah said loud enough to cause concern.

"What's wrong?" Marco asked.

"Raheem done called my phone ten times. I had it on vibrate."

When Marco entered the living room Farrah's eyes were consumed with fear.

"Just tell him you had the music up too loud to hear your phone on vibrate."

Farrah shook her head dismissing his idea because she knew how her boyfriend was. It was never that simple when she wasn't available for him. He would immediately accuse her of something.

"Where's the washcloth and stuff? I gotta go."

She wanted to birdbath in the sink to save time, but she was sweaty all over and needed a shower. She wanted to call him back now, but didn't want Marco to hear the conversation knowing it might get heated. She grabbed the towels, wrapping one around her hair and hopped in the shower washing her body as quick as she could. *Why was he calling her like crazy when he was supposed to be with his friends?* She dried herself off and got dressed in the middle of the hallway where she'd left her sundress. Marco stood by silently still admiring her body in the mist or her turmoil.

"Is everything gonna be okay?" he finally said.

"I hope so," Farrah replied as she fixed her hair and slid into her sandals.

She glanced at her phone and saw Raheem had called again."

"It'll be okay," Marco assured her.

"Whatever, if I'm not at work Monday, you know I'm dead."

"Don't even play like that."

As Farrah flung her purse over her shoulder Marco pulled her close and kissed her goodbye. She returned his kiss and dashed for the door, leaving it open as she fled the apartment in haste. Once she was inside her jeep she nervously returned Raheem's call.

"Why the fuck you ain't answering your fucking phone!" Raheem yelled.

"I didn't hear it, it was in my purse on vibrate," she yelled back quite convincingly.

"Where the fuck you at?"

"Stop yelling at me!"

"I'm a yell all the fuck I want until I find out why you couldn't answer your phone for a whole hour."

"I just told you it was in my purse."

"Yeah right, who you think you talking to?"

"Why wouldn't I answer the phone, Raheem, if I heard it ringing?"

"That's what I wanna know, and you still ain't told me where the fuck you at?"

"I'm on my way home."

"Coming from where?"

"Do I question you?" she fired back.

"Oh, that's how you gon' play? Huh? Bi...you know what? Come on home, I'll be there waiting on you."

Click

Raheem hung up on her.

"Shit!" she vented.

Farrah considered calling him back but decided it would only make her seem guilty of something if she continued to over explain herself. The truth was she could remember vividly on more than one occasion when Raheem didn't answer his phone for long periods at a time, so she had a leg to stand on. She drove home afraid but still not feeling the least bit guilty about her actions. Farrah believed if Raheem was treating her right, there would be no need to step outside of their relationship and that was the bottom line. She parked in the front of the house instead of the driveway. If things got too intense she wanted to make sure they both had a clear path to leave the house. Their son was away with her family so she knew Raheem wouldn't hold back or bite his tongue. When she walked in the house Raheem was sitting at the dining room table with a cold blank stare in his eyes.

"I'm gonna ask you one last time, Farrah, where was you at?"

"I was with my girlfriend from work at her house. I left my phone downstairs in my purse and we was upstairs the whole time. I told you I get tired of sitting in this house by myself."

"And I know that, that why I went and bought these tickets to surprise your stupid ass, but you went and fucked that all up."

"Don't talk to me like that," Farrah complained as she spotted the tickets to her favorite movie theater with inside dining. As she glanced back and forth from Raheem to the tickets that lay on the dining room table she began to feel bad...really, really bad. Raheem had told her that he was hanging out with friends only to try and surprise her with a date.

Chapter 17

By the time Marco returned to the morning shift, it seemed Farrah had somehow managed to smooth things out at home and they continued on like nothing ever happened. The bond they shared was continuously growing and the sexual energy between them was even hotter and heavier. There was obvious tension between Marco and Kevin, but they seemed to be cordial on the surface. Some of their coworkers began to give them constant judgmental glances as Farrah and Marco openly flaunted their creeping around at work. It wasn't abnormal for someone to walk up and catch them hugged up or kissing when they thought no one was around to see.

At the time clock sometimes Farrah would stand in front of Marco in the congested crowd leaving no space between them as her booty brush slyly and gently up against his manhood. They had no shame and it was becoming evident that at least one person was become increasingly agitated by it all. Their physical relationship had brought them closer together and now it was like they couldn't keep their hands off of each other. One day, around Sweetest Day, Kevin saw Farrah and Marco exchanging what looked to be gifts before they went their separate ways.

"Yo' Marco," Kevin called out.

"What's up?" Marco said as he approached Kevin.

"Need to holla at you," Kevin said as he pulled Marco to the side away from everyone getting ready to clock out.

Farrah glanced back at the exchange as she was exiting the building wondering what it was about.

"What's going on?" Marco asked.

"Been getting some complaints about inappropriate behavior at the job, between you and Farrah," Kevin lied.

"Inappropriate behavior?"

"Yeah man, you know it ain't my business, but the word got back to me."

Marco couldn't believe one word of what he was hearing.

"I see inappropriate behavior from everybody in this muthafucka so how we get singled out?"

It was well known that all the married men in the front office had side chicks at the job. He'd seen it with his own eyes and doubted if his relationship with Farrah had reached the front office. Something wasn't sitting right about it at all.

"Yeah I guess they say y'all getting a little too close for comfort around here. You know I ain't trying to chastise you or nothing, but as a supervisor it's my job to give you the verbal warning."

"Fuck that shit my nigga, they ain't talking about nothing. Tell your bosses if they got a problem with me they can come holla at me," Marco said showing contempt for his authority. "Anything else, though?"

Kevin stood there wide-eyed in complete disbelief.

"Naw man that's it I guess."

Marco turned his back and walked away. He just wasn't buying the bologna that Kevin was selling. There was just too much going on at the job for him to believe someone besides him was so upset that they went to the front office and complained. He was really starting to dislike Kevin more and more each day. Later on that day Farrah called just to be nosey and get the scoop on what the whole conversation was about.

"He starting to be quite a character," Farrah said referring to Kevin.

"He starting to make me wanna smack the shit out of 'em."

"You know, it's something I never told you about Kevin."

"What's that?" Marco questioned.

"Yeah, remember when he first sent you on second shift?"

"Yeah, what about it?"

"He called himself trying to talk to me as soon as you wasn't around," she informed.

"Word?"

"Hell yeah, but this not even his first time trying to get on. He tried to get on some years back when I first started at the job."

"So I guess his feelings hurt that I came through and got the one that got away from him, huh?"

"I don't know, but that sounds about right. Whatever it is, we should just be a little more discreet from here on out. I don't want either one of us getting no write-ups."

"Agreed," Marco said.

"So you still going to the company party?" Farrah asked changing subjects.

Just then Marco heard Nae turning her key in the door and seconds later she and Mariah came strolling in.

"Yeah, I heard it was off the hook last year. I'm looking forward to it," Marco said playing it cool.

"Why you couldn't wash none to these dishes?" Nae complained.

"Because this ain't my house. My dishes clean," Marco shot back.

"Well, I see your main thang just came in, so I guess I'll see you tomorrow," Farrah said.

"Alright homey," Marco said making sure he ended the call as if he were talking to one of his homeboys.

Nae came into the kitchen with Marco and began putting some of the groceries away she'd just bought.

"So what was off the chain that you looking forward to?" she pried.

"This party my job has every year."

"Oh, that sounds fun, I wanna go."

Marco was stumped for a minute, but he was thinking no way in hell Nae was going to this party.

"You couldn't waiting to see if I was gonna invite you or not, instead of just inviting yourself?" he said out of frustration.

Nae's face was all disfigured at the moment.

"I just said I wanna go damn, is that a problem?"

"I didn't say it was a problem, but you ain't even gonna know nobody there."

"So...you can't introduce me to some of your coworkers, I'm not understanding?"

Marco just leaned against the doorway silently wishing she wouldn't have walked in when she did. He certainly didn't mind hanging out with Nae, but no way was he putting her and Farrah in the same room together.

"Fuck it, I don't even wanna go no more," Nae finally said after seeing her presence wasn't wanted.

"You can go, I don't care," he lied after seeing she was turned off by his actions.

"You don't even sound like you want me to go."

Marco fell silent again as she stared into his eyes searching for the truth. "Whatever," Nae said slamming the jar of spaghetti sauce down hard on the counter before making her dramatic exit from the kitchen.

Chapter 18

The day of the company party came quickly and Marco was beyond pissed because Nae was still trying to tag along with him. She had already paid for a babysitter and everything. The problem was, now that she knew about the party, he couldn't think of any reasonable explanation to tell her she was uninvited. He thought about just telling her the party was canceled, but he knew that unless he stayed home with her all night, she'd never believe him. From his apartment, Marco tried picking false fights with her over the phone.

"Stop smacking in my goddamn ear like you crazy," he complained

"I'm sorry, I'm hungry, damn."

"Sorry nothing, that shit is so unladylike...stupid ass," he added just to get a rise.

In the end, none of it seemed to work and Nae's plans didn't change. It was like her mind was locked on her destination for the evening and nothing was going to detour her. The only logical escape plan he could conjure up was to just simply turn his phone off and not show up to pick Nae up, and then just go to the party alone. He would have to come up with some elaborate lie that she probably wouldn't believe anyway. Yes, he would have to face the music the next day, but anything would be better than having both the women in his life in the same room.

****

Job-related events were the only time Farrah and Marco got to hang out together in public. She was looking forward to tonight and she knew Marco was as well. She wore a sexy red, thigh-high, spaghetti-strap dress and red heels. Her lengthy hair was bone straight with a part down the middle. The slit designs in the front of her dress made her breast jump out at unsuspecting eyes.

"Damn baby, you look so good I almost wanna make you stay home with me," Raheem said as he eased up behind her in the mirror wrapping his arms around her waist.

"I'll wake you up when I get back if you want me to," Farrah said as he kissed the back of her neck.

"Please do," Raheem responded.

He wanted to complain about her dress until he remembered he was the one who bought it. Besides that, his woman had a banging body that you just couldn't hide and he was glad he had it all to himself.

"I'm bout to go, give me a kiss," Farrah said as she turned to face him.

"Two drink minimum," he reminded her after they kissed.

"Right," she agreed just for his peace of mind.

Fatima rode shotgun as Farrah drove to the hall.

"That boy Marco gon' be there?" Fatima asked.

"Mmm hmm," Farrah said smiling at the thought.

Her sister caught on to her delight.

"You is in love with that nigga," she teased.

"It's fucked up, but I really am. I love them both. I love what I have at home; you know my family means the world to me but...I feel like I'm in too deep with Marco now. I love what we have and how he treats me. He makes me feel special in so many ways."

"Well, just be smart about it, that's all I can say."

"You think I'm being selfish?"

"Maybe a little, but I understand once feelings are involved it can be hard to let go."

"Exactly! How do you let go of your best friend? Your only friend?"

"So Raheem is not your friend?"

"No, Raheem is my man."

Fatima just shook her head and left it alone.

****

Farrah passed her tickets to the lady behind the booth and the two of them headed inside. She was fashionably late so most of her coworkers had already arrived. She found a table where most of the girls she got along with were all sitting together.

"Hey everybody," she spoke and waved as she sat her bottle of Ciroc down and began to unbutton her leather blazer.

After hanging her blazer on the back of her chair she immediately began to scan the room for Marco.

"Yup he here," she heard Tia say.

"Who?" Farrah asked playing dumb.

"You know who," Tia said.

"Know I don't," Farrah said getting a little annoyed.

That's the reason I don't like bitches because they never know how to mind their own business, she thought. Fatima could tell what Farrah was thinking and decided to make them both some drinks before they started the night off on the wrong foot. Moments later Marco popped up at the table.

"Whassup?" he spoke to everyone at the table.

Farrah could tell he was buzzing already as she peered at the cup in his hand.

"What you sipping on?"

"I'm on that Hennessy tonight. It ain't holding me up either," he chuckled.

Marco wore a dark blue casual button up and dark denim jeans. He looked good and Farrah wanted to kiss him on the lips.

"You look like you having a good time," she acknowledged.

"Aye, it's a party, ain't that's what we came to do? Huh? Get on my level!" he encouraged talking trash.

"Oh, I'm about to," Farrah said as she took a big sip from her first drink.

It wasn't long before the dance floor was packed with people enjoying the night the same as the last time they'd all partied together. Once Farrah was firmly intoxicated, she was ready to join them. Fatima had met a guy and was in a deep conversation. She went to find Marco to see if he would dance with her, but she ended up bumping into Kevin first.

"Hey sexy lady, you looking good tonight," he flirted.

"Hey, thanks," she responded.

"What's up, you wanna dance?" Kevin offered.

"Umm," she stalled as she scanned the room for Marco and spotted him approaching. "I was just looking for you," Farrah said.

"Well, here I am."

Kevin was still waiting on an answer from Farrah as if he didn't get the memo. Farrah looked back and forth from Kevin to Marco.

"You mind if I dance with Kev-"

"Hell yeah, I mind," Marco cutting her off before she could finish the sentence.

Farrah burst into laughter finding his jealousy hilarious while Kevin just turned and walked away feeling foolish. Marco moved closer to her and stroked her hair. "You look more beautiful every day," he said loudly over the music.

Farrah was still smiling as her laughter had just ended.

"You know, sometimes I feel like I really do have two boyfriends," she admitted.

"Well, you don't. You have a boyfriend and a best friend. There's a big difference."

"And that is?"

"Relationships don't always last, but real friends do."

"But...I'm in love with you."

"I'm in love with you too. It is what it is."

After that exchange, Farrah grabbed Marco by that hand and lead him to the dance floor where she gave him a standing lap dance even dirtier than the one before. She would never dance like that for Raheem for fear he would never look at her as the sweet and innocent girl he wanted to spend the rest of his life with again. That's when she realized Marco was right. There was a big difference in her boyfriend and her best friend. For some reason, she felt totally free with Marco and she could just let go of all of her inhibitions.

After they got burned out on the dance floor everyone began to click up and take pictures on the stage. Marco and Farrah joined in and took about ten group photos before the crowd of coworkers dispersed.

"Hey let's take one, just me and you," Marco suggested.

'Nah, that's evidence," Farrah giggled.

"Nah, I'll take it home and put it away where nobody would ever find it."

"Alright, come on," Farrah agreed as they headed back to the stage.

The two posed in each other's arms as if they were the couple that just won best dressed or something. There was no need to be discreet here, everyone already knew about them. When Marco spotted Kevin looking on in the crowd, he grabbed Farrah's ass in as the cameraman snapped the picture, just to add insult to injury. As soon as the flash was out of his eyes Marco looked out into the crowd again and spotted Nae and her girl Tamara maneuvering through the crowd, coming straight at him. He wished he knew where the back door exit was at so he could make a run for it. Nae had hacked into his Facebook account and searched all his friend's pages until she found out where the party was being held.

"Maaaan," Marco said sounding defeated.

"What's wrong?" Farrah asked as they exited the stage.

"My baby mama here," he warned.

"What?" Farrah said in disbelief.

"Yeah, just walk away," he said calmly as Nae came within a few feet of them.

"Don't try to get rid of that hoe now, I just saw you with your hand all over her ass!" Nae attacked.

Farrah was about to keep walking, but then she remembered this wasn't the first time Nae had disrespected her and she wasn't going to keep allowing it. She went back to confront her.

"Bitch you don't know me to be disrespecting me," Farrah lashed.

"What bitch?" Nae said as she went to charge Farrah, but Marco jumped in between them.

"You better get your girl, Marco," Fatima warmed as she came up behind her sister.

"This is why you ain't want me to come huh? So you could be up in here acting like you single? You got me fucked up," Nae ranted.

"You better calm the fuck down!"

By now Fatima and Tamara had begun exchanging threats and name calling. It was Fatima who struck first by tossing her drink in Tamara's face and splashing Nae as well.

"Oh hell naw," Nae shouted as she charged at the sisters and Tamara followed.

Marco couldn't hold them both and Nae broke free long enough to take a swing at Farrah who had Tamara's hair in her hand as she fought Fatima. The punch only connected slightly and then the guys all stepped in and helped Marco pull them apart quickly. That's when Marco turned and picked Nae up completely off of her feet and tossed her over his shoulder to carry her outside.

"Put me down, Marco!" Nae screamed as they headed towards the exit with Tamara trailing behind still cursing Fatima out.

 Farrah and Fatima watched them leave as they began being questioned by Farrah's coworkers about the incident.

"You okay?" Farrah asked Fatima.

"Yeah, I'm straight that bitch ain't do nothing to me."

"Come on, it's time to go," Farrah said still rattled and frustrated.

It seemed the party was going back to normal as Farrah's coworkers continued to come over and check on her one by one. Farrah was headed to get her jacket when she spotted the cameraman and remembered the picture they had just taken before the fight broke out. She went back to the area where he was stationed. She paid for the picture and then gave it to Fatima with strict orders.

"Take this muthafucka home and burn it!"

"Gotcha."

****

After having Nae pinned to the side of his truck for over five minutes, Marco was able to finally talk her down. It was a night that started out so beautiful, but had turned into a nightmare and he just wanted it to be over badly. He told Tamara to drive Nae's car home while Nae rode with him so they could talk.

"I knew you would do this to me. I knew it, I knew it, I fucking knew it!" Nae claimed on the ride home.

"Nae I think you knew I didn't want to be in a relationship fresh out of jail."

"Then why agree to one?"

"Actually, I never really did, the shit just happened because I knew that's what you really wanted."

"Really? You gon' sit up here and say that to me?" Nae said shooting daggers his way as her heart got heavy. "So you was never happy?"

"I'm not saying that at all. Just because I didn't want to jump into a relationship doesn't mean I don't love you. I love you Nae."

"How many times are you gonna break my heart and then turn around and tell me you love me?"

"First of all, taking a picture with someone is not breaking your heart."

Nae grew furious. She was seconds away from punching him but realized he was driving and it would put her in danger.

"You fucking turned your phone off and stood me up, you grimy son-of-a-bitch! You gon' sit up here and try to tell me that's not your bitch? Huh? You gon' look me in my face and keep lying?"

"What I'm saying is, I do love you, and I don't want to be away from you and my daughter."

"Well that's too bad, you should've thought about that before you decided you was gon' be Sweet Dick Willie. Play time is over. "

****

The next morning Farrah was up vomiting her guts out in the toilet until she had nothing left to give. She couldn't understand why her stomach was so upset knowing she hadn't had much to drink after her night was cut short by drama. As she dry heaved over the porcelain, she began to believe she just might be revisiting the familiar feeling of morning sickness. By noon she still didn't feel well and decided to just go get a pregnancy test to clear her mind of that thought.

Raheem was out and about all morning so she had to take her son with her. When they arrived back at home, she told him to go and take a nap while she locked herself in the bathroom and took the test. If she was pregnant she knew Raheem would be overjoyed. He was looking forward to having another child, but Farrah had planned to wait until they were married. As she waited, the thought of Marco and the night they went unprotected crossed her mind.

"Oh God," she mumbled then shook off the fear that was lingering.

As she glanced at the stick and it confirmed her pregnancy her fear slowly returned. She immediately began to reprimand herself for not being more responsible. With things like the morning after pill readily available, there was absolutely no reason why should have to question who she was pregnant by.

With all the madness of last night and now this, she knew it was time to run as far away from Marco as she could. Things had certainly gotten way out of hand. After about twenty minutes of throwing herself a pity party, Farrah pulled it together and came out of the bathroom.

She went into the bedroom and began to prepare a basket of dirty laundry to wash. She heard Raheem come in and heart sank to her stomach at the thought of telling him the news. His footsteps sounded extremely heavy as he stomped to the bedroom. He had to be angry about something.

"Farrah!" he shouted, startling her as she stopped sorting out clothes and stood straight up.

As soon as she spotted Raheem the rage in his eyes said it all. She knew that somehow, he knew. Raheem busted in the door and smacked Farrah so hard she fell onto the bed. He climbed on top of her and wrapped his big hands around her throat. "You been cheating on me bitch?" he accused.

"No, what's wrong with you?" Farrah screams in a strained voice from being choked.

"Don't lie to me, I will fucking kill you right now!"

"I'm not lying, I swear. Let me go!"

"You taking pictures with a nigga hand all over your ass? Huh? Explain that bitch!"

Farrah pried his fingers back just enough to get some air circulating through her lungs. Raheem realized he was actually cutting off her air supply in his jealous rage so he took one hand from around her throat and cocked his fist back.

"Raheem I didn't do it, whatever it is, please just let me talk."

Raheem stared her in the eyes with his fist still in position. "Please Raheem, just let me talk."

He got off of her and searched for his cell phone. Once he found it, he thumbed through the phone until he found the picture. He threw his phone at Farrah and it hit her in her thigh.

"Explain this shit! Tell me how you gon' explain that?"

Farrah's mind raced as she grabbed the phone and stared at her undoing. Somehow, Raheem had gotten a hold of the photo of Farrah and Marco posed up like a couple at the party. At first, Farrah was so stunned no words would formulate in her mind to speak aloud. She soon realized that silence could be deadly in a situation like this. She needed to say something; anything.

"Listen, I was drunk and…"

"So that what the fuck you finna tell me? You was drunk?"

"Let me finish, please. I was drunk so I didn't realize his hand was on my ass because he did that at the last minute. By the time I realized the picture was already taken. We got into a big fight about it right after and I swear, I was just praying that nobody would ever see the picture. That's why I came back home so early because after we got into it about the picture, I left."

Half-truths mixed with a pack of lies had given Farrah some breathing room as Raheem mulled over her story.

"Why the fuck you take a picture with this nigga anyway? You ain't supposed to be flicking up with niggas in the first place."

"Everybody was taking pictures, if you saw that one then you should have seen the rest of them. I told the

Cameraman to throw that shit in the garbage because it's disrespectful as hell," she lied.

"Well, he didn't fucking throw it away, he put it on the internet for the world to see. And I don't give a fuck if everybody in the club took pictures you ain't have no business taking a picture hugged up with no nigga. I should slap the fuck out you!" Raheem vented as he paced the room.

"I know it was wrong Raheem but..."

Boom!

Raheem punched the wall so hard he put a hole right through it. "Look, I'm sorry it was nothing like that I swear. I swear to God!" she continued begging out of fear for her wellbeing as well as losing her relationship.

"I would have never disrespected you like that," Raheem yelled.

"I wasn't trying to be disrespectful."

"What do you call it bitch?"

Farrah was wishing she could find the cameraman and shoot him for posting that picture after seeing all the trouble it caused at the party.

"Raheem, we've been together for eight years and I've never disrespected you. I know this looks bad, but I was drunk and it's not what it looks like. I would never do that to you."

Raheem couldn't stand the sound of her trembling voice as tears streamed down her face. He stormed out of the room and out of the house slamming the door so hard it shook the entire foundation.

Chapter 19

Raheem didn't spend the night with Farrah. He came back home a few hours later, just to pack some things and leave again. It was the first time in years they didn't sleep in the same bed, but Farrah was so afraid to ignite his fire again, she didn't try to stop him from leaving. She knew that more than likely, he would be at his mom's or his sister's house. In a conversation with Raheem's sister, Farrah learned that his best friend was the one that snitched on her. He'd spotted the photographer's pictures on Facebook, and when he spotted Farrah in some of the pictures he zoomed in only to get hit with a rude awakening. He immediately called Raheem over to let him see it with his own eyes.

The photographer was only trying to promote himself, but in the process, he had turned Farrah's world upside down. Deep down, she knew she had no one to blame, but it didn't stop her wanting the picture man on a cold slab. She was too terrified to reach out to Marco because of everything that had happened in a twenty-four-hour time span, so she waited for Monday morning at work to reach out to him. They both showed up for work extra early knowing they had so much to discuss, but Marco only knew the half. Soon as she saw his truck pull into the lot she called his cell phone.

"Can you park over here next to me?" she asked.

"Yeah," Marco agreed.

Farrah got out of her jeep and jumped in the truck with Marco. The parking lot was still almost empty with the exception of two other cars parked down by the entrance. The mood was extremely awkward for the first time ever as Farrah wore a face of stone.

"I know you mad and I know this fucked up everything big time, but I didn't tell her to come," Marco explained.

"Look, fuck your baby mama, my nigga knows."

"What?" Marco said in shock.

"I mean, he thinks he knows. He saw the picture we took with your hand all over my ass."

"How the hell did he see that?"

"That stupid ass picture man took it from his camera and put it on the internet. All of the pictures we took at the party are on Facebook and Instagram."

"Get the fuck outta here!"

"I swear to God."

"What he say to you about it?"

"He didn't say shit at first; he came through the door and straight smack the shit out of me, then starting explaining why he did it."

"Damn," Marco said feeling bad for her. "Then what happened?"

"Well, after he stopped choking me, he showed me the picture in his phone. Then he just started snapping and pacing and punching walls and shit."

"Damn, I'm so sorry."

"He cursed me out so bad, and he made me feel like I wasn't shit."

"You know I would never do nothing to break up your happy home," Marco assured her.

"Well, you just did. He packed a bag and left, and I been trying to get him to come back home ever since."

"Is he trying to work it out? I mean, do you think you can make this right?"

"I don't know man. He just feels so disrespected, and he's still very upset. We have to end this now, Marco. I love you, but I can't lose my family, and I know you don't wanna lose yours."

"I understand and you're right. I need to try and fixed things with Nae, and it's not gonna be easy at all."

"No calls, no texting, no flirting at work; I'm done," Farrah confirmed.

"I know you're serious and I'm serious too. Shit, the nigga know what I look like now. You think I wanna be walking around watching my back? As much as I love you, and I know it's gonna be hard losing my best friend, nothing last forever."

"Right," Farrah agreed. "And there's one more thing."

"What's that?"

"Are you one thousand percent sure you didn't make any mistakes that time we didn't use protection?"

Marco thought back to the blissful night that was almost a painful thought now under the circumstances. He remembered pulling out for sure, but there was no way he could be one thousand percent sure of anything. He went ahead and told Farrah what she needed to hear at the time.

"I'm positive, why you ask?"

"Because I'm pregnant," she explained.

"Oh wow!"

"So I'm gonna ask you again. Are you..."

"Farrah, I'm positive."

"Okay," Farrah said feeling a little better now."

"Does he know?"

"No. I only found out like a half hour before the big bang."

"Maybe you should tell him before he tries to kill you again," Marco teased trying not to end things on a sour note.

"That shit ain't funny. Let me go before all these gossiping muthafuckas pull up. I know they gon' have a lot to talk about today."

"Right, I heard they been on Facebook talking about we ruined the party."

"Are you serious?" Farrah said in disbelief.

"I wish I wasn't," Marco said shaking his head.

"I know it ain't nobody but them bitches. That's why I don't like bitches," Farrah said before she opened the door.

****

The work day was a difficult one, to say the least. As Farrah tried to make it through the day, she could feel the gossip in the air. It seemed like every time she walked by she'd spot someone whispering to someone else. She knew they were probably talking about her and Marco, but there was no way to prove it so she just ignored them. On her break, she decided to eat outside in her jeep. She was in no mood to deal with her fake ass coworkers, not even the ones she got along with. In times like this, no one could be trusted. She saw Marco sitting in his car also probably feeling the same way.

She wondered would it be like this forever with them avoiding each other and everyone else. After she ate Farrah went on Facebook to see if she could find the comments about her and Marco ruining the party. She roamed on a few pages of some of the coworkers that she knew never really cared for her. They were the prime suspects. To her surprise, she didn't find anything negative said about her or Marco. When she went to her coworker's pages that she was friendly with that's when she saw the post from the day after the party.

The party was off the chain until all that drama broke out. Farrah scrolled through the comments.

:We was having a good time until you know what

:smh

:Yeah Farrah and n'em kinda ruin the night with that bullshit

Farrah was heated and felt like she was being attacked.

"Bitch I didn't ruin shit, y'all hoes was still partying when I left," she screamed at her phone.

She sat there for a minute deciding if she should address what was said. She read all the comments again, remembering who said what. Just then she realized she could use the negativity to her advantage. This proved that she was in some sort of altercation at the party, and she desperately needed Raheem to believe that. She took a screen shot of the post and the comments and sent it to Raheem. She added a message.

Farrah: I told you there was a big incident that took place after that picture. Maybe now you will believe me.

This had to work. The comments didn't say anything about the incident except the fact that she was involved. This would allow her to create her own version of what really happened. She knew it was playing with fire, but with her relationship on the ropes, she had to chance it. Raheem called her minutes later.

"Hello?" Farrah answered.

"So, that nigga put his hands on you or something?"

"No it didn't go that far, it was just a bunch of shouting back and forth."

"So he disrespected you?" Raheem asked angrily.

Farrah didn't know how to answer that question. She hadn't thought it through on how this might affect Marco, she was only thinking of saving her relationship.

"Look, it's over and done with now."

"Not if that nigga disrespected you it ain't. You know I ain't going for that shit."

"It was just a argument okay? I took care of it."

"Naw, fuck that. He had no business putting his hand all over your ass like that in the first place. I'm coming up there, and I want you to point this nigga out."

"No Raheem, don't come up here," Farrah pleaded, but Raheem had already hung up. "Oh God!" she vented.

In a matter of minutes, Farrah had managed to turn a bad situation worse. She couldn't think straight as she watched Marco head back to the building as their lunch break came to an end. She had to stop Raheem from coming to her job. She knew nothing good could come from it, but she also knew he was crazy enough to do it. She called him back.

"Hello?" he answered still sounding pissed off.

"Raheem you cannot come up here clowning okay? You could get me fired," she reasoned.

"I'm not coming up there to clown. I just wanna talk to him."

"Talk about what? I told you it's over and done with," Farrah yelled.

"Why the fuck you trying so hard to protect this nigga?"

"I'm not trying to protect shit, but my job, and you should be trying to do the same."

"It's too late now, I just walked off my job site, and I'm on my way up there. I'll call you when I'm outside."

"Raheem no!" she pleaded, but he hung up again.

She tried calling him back, but he never answered again. Her break was over, and she would be late getting back to her post, but it didn't matter right now.

She would explain to her supervisor later. Right now she had to stop Raheem because if she didn't, she may not have a job tomorrow. She rushed through the front entrance and found the security guard.

"Hey listen, I need a favor," she told him.

"What's that?"

"My boyfriend's name is Raheem. If he comes up here do not let him inside. Have someone page me, and I'll come up front, but do not let him come in."

"Gotcha," the guard agreed.

With that handled, Farrah hurried back to her station. She felt all the eyes on her, followed by whispers of speculation as she passed by. Her supervisor was standing by her station waiting for her to arrive. She made up a lie about her boyfriend being locked out of the house and on his way to pick up her house keys. Farrah was an excellent worker who never caused any problems, so her supervisor bought her story and went on his way. Now all she had to do was stop Raheem and Marco from bumping heads.

She worked harder and faster than normal as her mind raced, and the clock ticked the minutes away bringing the possibility of confrontation just that much closer. As time passed, she realized if he was really on his way, he should have arrived by now. After another few more minutes passed she heard the ding of text message alert on her phone. She stopped working long enough to sneak a peek at it knowing it could be Raheem and it was.

Raheem: I guess you was right. I should've stayed put because I just got into a car accident but I'm okay.

Farrah couldn't help but feel a little relieved that her boyfriend was in a car accident. She had to look up in at the ceiling and thank God for his divine intervention.

Chapter 20

Things were going well for Marco financially. He had just been given his first raise and even won a small amount of cash at the casino over the weekend. On the other hand, his personal life was in shambles. He and Farrah weren't speaking at all and Nae would only talk to him if it was pertaining to Mariah. It had been a rough week, but he was thankful for the things that were going well in his life. He was walking parole down and could finally see the end coming near.

When Friday came, all he wanted to do was go pick up Mariah and spend some time with her. Just like Farrah, Marco had been aware of the gossip that was all around him all week. It seemed his haters were in celebration of his misfortune. But the job paid well and kept him out of trouble so he wasn't about to let anyone stand in his way; especially Kevin. It seemed as if Kevin had been increasing his workload since he was given a mandatory raise. It was always something that Kevin was doing that seemed a little personal. Sometimes it was little nitpicking and other times it was piling on more work than necessary.

Marco spotted Farrah headed to the time clock, and he unconsciously headed to the restroom to avoid her. It wasn't so much that he wanted to avoid her, but the onslaught of attention they drew now when they were around each other was uncomfortable for both of them. Everyone wanted to know what was going on with the two that were once like bread and butter. But since neither was the type to put their business in the streets, all people could do was assume. The line at the clock was moving super slow considering it was Friday. When Marco finished using the restroom the line was still long and Farrah was still in it.

There were three guys behind Farrah including Kevin. When Kevin saw Marco approaching he tapped the two guys on the shoulder and whispered something. The two guys stepped out of line with a look of confusion on their faces. It didn't take long for Marco to realize that Kevin was hoping to see some fireworks between him and Farrah, or he wanted to make them uncomfortable. He'd never seen so much bitchassness in his entire life. He wanted to just go off and start smacking niggas starting with Kevin, but he maintained his cool as he stepped up and stood behind Farrah. She was at the time clock now, and after punching out they exchanged glances.

"Hey," she spoke.

"Hey," he spoke back before Farrah sped off leaving the spectators disappointed.

Marco punched out.

"Good thing y'all didn't get no popcorn for that bullshit huh?" he said as he walked away.

It was good to know that he and Farrah were at least on speaking terms. He felt bad about what he'd put her through, but it was too weird to keep walking around ignoring each other every day. All Marco really wanted was to be an improvement on Farrah's existing life and to make sure she was happy. He was willing to let her go if it would bring peace to her home. Still, as he watched her leave the building he zoomed in on that amazing ass, switching away he knew it was going to be a crushing blow to accept that it was gone forever.

When Marco made it outside he realized that Farrah wasn't driving her jeep. There was a man behind the wheel, and as soon as he spotted Marco they locked eyes. The stare down that transpired was so intense he knew it had to Raheem. He looked over at Farrah who sat in the passenger seat with her head down, eyes glued to the floor. As Raheem pulled away slowly, not once did the two men break eye contact. Never one to back down, Marco decided right then that if Raheem wanted trouble he was going to get it. He would not be spared because of Farrah if Raheem bought drama his way.

****

Things were still very rocky with Farrah and Raheem. After the car crash, Raheem was fired from his job for walking off the site and he blamed Farrah. His car was still in the collision shop, and he had to pay a huge deductible which made matters worse. Although he'd promised Farrah he wouldn't confront Marco, it was killing his pride to look him in the eyes and not address the disrespect.

"That was him wasn't it," he barked at Farrah as they rode home.

Farrah didn't respond. "You didn't hear me talking to you? If I ever find out you was fucking him I'm gonna go to jail. I'm telling you that right now."

With so much going on, Farrah had held back her pregnancy news hoping for better timing to make the announcement. But with Raheem breathing down her neck about Marco, she couldn't think of a better time to change his thought process and the entire conversation.

"I'm pregnant," she blurted.

"What?"

"You heard me. I'm pregnant."

"How you know?"

"I took a test."

"When?"

"Yesterday," Farrah lied.

"So why you ain't tell me yesterday?"

"I wanted to tell you, but we kept arguing all day because you keep blaming me for losing your fucking job. Didn't nobody tell you to walk off your job, I told you to stay."

"You right," Raheem finally admitted.

At the moment, he was certainly glad he hadn't done anything stupid to cost Farrah her job. She was going to need her job now more than ever, and he would have to find work fast. Preparing for a child was costly, but deep down Raheem was excited even though he refused to show it at the time. "You made a doctor's appointment yet?"

"Yeah, it's next week."

Farrah could sense that Raheem was excited about another baby. It was something they had always agreed they wanted even if it wasn't under the circumstances Farrah had hope for. This would hopefully bring them closer again.

****

After work, Marco went home and changed clothes then picked up his daughter for their movie date. Nae was a little more cordial now that she'd had some time to cool down. Marco wanted to try and work things out with her, but didn't want his words to fall on deaf ears, so he waited. Meanwhile, he enjoyed the alone time with Mariah. The kid's movie put Marco to sleep at the theater, but he could tell Mariah was all in right before he fell asleep. After the movie, he called his mom to see if she was doing okay, and if she wanted to see Mariah. She was elated.

"You wanna go see your granny?" Marco asked as the got in the truck.

"I always wanna see my granny," Mariah assured him.

"Well excuse me for asking li'l mama."

"Daddy."

"What's up?"

"Why you don't spend the night at our house anymore?"

"Because your mama mad at me, and she think I'm a dirty dog."

"Well, is you a dirty dog, daddy?"

"No, I'm not. Do you think I am?"

"No, I don't think so."

"Good, well, you should call your mom and tell her that."

"Okay," Mariah agreed.

Marco started it as a joke between him and Mariah but then decided to follow through with it. He dialed Nae's number and handed Mariah the phone.

"What?" Nae answered expecting Marco.

"Mama?"

"Oh, hey baby."

"I'm calling to tell you that my daddy is not a dirty dog."

"What?" Nae giggled.

"Yeah, at least I don't think he so."

"When did you ever hear me call your daddy that?"

"Never, but he said that's why he don't spend the night no more."

"Give your daddy the phone," Nae ordered.

Marco was chuckling as Mariah tried to intervene on his behalf. When she handed him the phone he wouldn't take it.

"Un un, I ain't in it. That's between you and your mama," he said loud enough for Nae to hear.

He was enjoying having Mariah as his go-between.

"He said..."

"I heard what he said, give your daddy the phone, and tell him I said stop playing."

Mariah did as she was told and handed Marco the phone.

"She said stop playing."

"Hello?" he finally answered.

"Now you know, I never bad mouth you to your daughter, so why would you sit up and tell her that?"

"I'm just messing around, Nae damn, why you gotta be so serious all the time?"

"Because I'm supposed to be serious in a serious situation," Nae said. "You playing with my heart is not a joke."

"I wasn't thinking that much into it, Nae, but you right and I'm sorry. I didn't wanna get you in a bad mood."

"I'm not in a bad mood, I'm fine."

"I just miss being with my family."

"I just bet you do," Nae said sarcastically.

"I'm dead serious. I broke it off with the girl, and I just want it to be me and you. I just wanna focus on us."

"She probably broke it off with your ass after seeing me act a fool. I really played myself that night. I should've just stayed my ass at home, but I knew something wasn't right."

"Say what you want, but I miss you, and I know you miss me."

The truth was Marco did miss his family being together, but he still wanted Farrah too, no matter how unlikely it seemed. He could only hope those feelings would pass, but if he couldn't have it all, hopefully, he could at least have his family.

"You know, maybe we shouldn't keep trying this relationship thing," Nae assessed. "Maybe we should just be friends and raise our daughter. You can see whoever you want, and I can see whoever I want. What you think?"

"Hell naw," Marco quickly disagreed.

That would mean he'd have to share the one girl that was all his and possibly lose her to someone else one day. No way he was willing to accept that.

"Why not? You said you weren't ready for a relationship, right?"

"Nae I just felt like we moved too fast out the gate. I know what I want now."

"Bye Marco."

Nae hung up before he could say anything else, but Marco was just glad to have had the conversation and get a chance to speak his mind. He knew Nae better than she knew herself, and eventually he would break down her walls of defense. He was always able to get in her head when he put his mind to it.

****

Farrah hated taking a day off work knowing they needed all the money they could get, but she had to keep her doctor's appointment. As she lay on the table, her primary care doctor took some blood then gave her a cup for a urine sample. She kept thinking of how stressed out Raheem had been since losing his job. They didn't have much money in savings and what they had would surely dwindle away when the bills came rolling in. Living off her income alone would be a tight fight. After confirming her last period the doctor made the announcement.

"So it looks like your about ten weeks along Ms. Nelson."

Farrah immediately did a reverse countdown back to when she and Marco had unprotected sex. It was right around ten weeks ago.

"Fuck!"

"Is something wrong?"

"No, my bad," she said playing it off.

Farrah and Raheem had an active sex life, so it was more than likely the baby was his, but the timing of her pregnancy left her with extreme concern. She couldn't have a baby by a man that wasn't Raheem. Her karma just couldn't be that fucked up. She cursed Marco inside her head for not having a condom that night. She cursed herself for being so stupid. She knew this situation would just aggravate her entire soul if she didn't talk to Marco about it again soon.

Chapter 21

As Nae continued to play hard to get, Marco found himself with a lot of free time on weekends. If he wasn't with Mariah, he usually found himself at home watching a game or thinking about Nae and Farrah. It was downright depressing sitting at home all alone on a Saturday night. It reminded him of prison too much. Trying to get his mind off of things, he decided to take a ride through his old stomping grounds where the strong devoured the weak, and the street soldiers played daily chess games with law enforcement. Every time he came through the hood it seemed like the scenery was altered in some way. Fewer houses and unfamiliar faces made his hood feel little more foreign each time.

When he turned on the block he used to hustle on, he spotted trap stars in the streets huddled around a dice game. Most had hoodies on with their backs turned so he couldn't see any faces yet. One man was recognizable even with his back turned because of his unique stance with his right shoulder perched high in the air and his left hand in his pocket. That was Carter for sure. Soon the gamblers could feel the presence of a car approaching, and they began to turn around and look one by one. They picked their money up off the ground and made way for the truck while peering inside at the driver. Marco spotted a few old friends in the crowd and pulled to the curb.

It was the same friends that could always lose a hundred in a dice game, but could put fifty on his books when he was doing hard time. Still, he held no grudges and was glad to see some of the dudes he'd shared so many memories with throughout his life. As he parked and hopped out Marco was greeted with love the same as always.

"Money Marco, what's up my nigga?" Carter spoke.

"You the money man," Marco returned after slapping fives with Carter and a few others.

"Niggas don't see you in the hood but every blue moon, what's good?" Carter continued.

"You know, I'm a working man now, so ain't no reason for me to be bending these blocks every day no more, you feel me?"

"Yeah, I feel that," Carter said as he went back to placing a bet on the dice.

Judging by their appearances, Marco could see the game was being good to some while destroying some others. Some of the hustlers were photo shoot fresh and glowing while others wore dingy outdated clothes, had old faces and graying hair. Dude in their late twenties were looking forty, and Marco knew it was the game taking its toll. Gone were the days where Marco viewed the trap star with the herculean heroism he once held. He had survived the game and he knew the ugly truth.

"What's up Marco, you want some of this?" his old friend Smurf said.

"Naw man I'm good, pass that Hennessy though."

Marco needed a stiff shot at the moment to take his mind off everything going on in his life. He took the bottle and the last remaining plastic cup that rested on top of it. He poured a straight shot with no chaser and continued to catch up with his old comrades. Carter was the first to look up and spot the two black

Crown Victoria unmarked police cars bending the block.

"Here they come, if got anything on you, better dip," Cater warned as the narcotics team approached.

Two men took off running through a field, while the others stayed put and pick their money up from the street. The first cop car took off driving through the field in pursuit of the men that ran. The second car pulled up right in front of the crowd and jumped out. Marco had just finished his drink before they hit the block. One black officer approached him directly.

"What's your name?"

Marco looked around.

"Who me?" he asked.

"Yeah you, come over here," the officer said as the other three began questioning all those who were brave enough to stick around. "You got anything in your pockets?"

"Just my money, my wallet and my keys," Marco replied.

Just then Marco started to panic. He'd forgotten that his gun was in the truck under the seat. He always took his gun when he went to the hood, just in case something went down. Now he was wishing like hell he'd just stayed home. If police searched his ride he was fucked.

"You live around here?"

"No, I don't. I used to."

"Yeah, looks like I seen you around here before," the cop said as he brought Marco over to the hood of the cop car and began to search him. "Whatchu doing out here? You a dopeboy?"

"No sir, I work five days a week," Marco answered.

"Oh yeah? You got a lot of money in your pocket, must be a good paying Job, huh?"

"Pays good enough."

The officer took Marco's driver's license and went to run his name through the system. Marco looked calm and collected on the outside, but he was seconds away from taking off running like the other dudes did. Police contact alone was a violation of his parole, but he kept reminding himself that he hadn't done anything and to just remain calm. It took about five minutes for the officer to run his name and come back. Everyone else had been searched and was now sitting on the curb awaiting directions from the police.

"You on parole?" the cop asked.

"Yeah."

"So you know you not supposed to be around other convicted felons right?"

"Yeah," Marco stated not giving him any more than necessary.

"I'm pretty sure it's at least three convicts out here in your little circle of friends."

Marco stood silently with his hands planted firmly on the hood, while the officer waited for his response. "Take this driver's license and get out of here man. I don't wanna see you on this block again, you hear me?"

"Yes sir," Marco agreed.

"If I catch you out here again, you going to jail," he assured Marco.

Marco took his identification and hurried off before the officer changed his mind. He took a deep breath as he started his truck and drove away. Driving home Marco thanked God the cops didn't search his truck and find the gun. A gun charge would have sent him right back to the belly of the beast from which he'd come. He soon realized how much the women in his life had been keeping him out of trouble. He couldn't slip up now, he'd come too far.

****

Monday morning during the first break, Farrah shot Marco a text. Her pregnancy and the timing were still heavy on her conscious.

Farrah: We need to talk it will only take a few minutes.

Marco: No problem, but what's it about?

Farrah: My pregnancy. Can I call you on our lunch break?

Marco: Of course

Farrah couldn't wait for noon so she could have this discussion one last time, and depending on how the conversation went, she might have a colossal decision to make. And as crazy as it was; as much as she hated to admit it, a part of her was eager to hear his voice again. When the lunch break came they both coincidentally pulled out of the parking lot behind each other. Farrah was glad Raheem had his car back so she could drive again. She had to be extra careful in the streets knowing he was unemployed, crazy, and had enough free time to try and watch her moves.

She called Marco as she drove behind him.

"Hey, what's up?" he answered.

"Hey, how are you?"

"I'm good, you been okay?"

"Yeah, I've been better, but I'm surviving."

"Sorry to hear that. I wish I could still be there for you," Marco said truthfully.

"I know, but don't remind me. Listen, I been to the doctor, and I'm like ten weeks pregnant. That means I got pregnant around the time we did you know what, and you know how. Even though I had a light period in September, it was basically just spotting. I didn't think much of it until after the party when I couldn't stop throwing up."

"I mean, not to be rude, but we talked about this already Farrah."

"I know, I know, but you have to understand; having a baby by another man would be like attempting suicide for me. I'm too young to die," she giggled, but inside she wasn't laughing. "He keeps telling me if he ever finds out I fucked around on him, he's going to jail."

"What does that supposed to mean?"

"What you think?"

"I don't know. Is he threatening me or is he threatening you? I seen the way the nigga was looking at me last week," he informed Farrah as they pulled alongside each other at a red light.

"Shit, I live with him, who you think he gonna go after first?" Farrah said as she glanced over at Marco and the both had to laugh at her comment.

"You gon' be good baby, don't stress over this."

Farrah sighed.

"Marco if there's even a tiny possibility that you slipped up just tell me now, and I swear I'm going to make an appointment to have an abortion immediately."

"How you gon' explain having an abortion?"

"Let me worry about that."

"Listen, I know how much your family means to you. I've never put you in jeopardy like that, you just gotta trust me on this one."

"You sound convincing," Farrah admitted.

"That's because I'm telling you the truth."

"Well thank you. You really help put my mind at ease a little bit."

"Glad I could help."

"Enjoy your lunch."

"But wait, don't hang up yet," Marco said as he pulled into a strip mall."

"What?"

"Tell me what else has you feeling so down?"

Farrah paused for a moment. This was her best friend and the one person she could always confide in. It just came so naturally to her that she couldn't deny herself the opportunity while she had it.

"It's everything. He got fired from his job for walking off the site. We constantly are bumping heads because of the incident with the picture which started everything. Now this pregnancy got me about to pull my hair out."

"Sounds like most of your problems revolve around me," Marco said sadly.

"I'm a grown woman, and I made my own decision. It's just becoming to be too stressful."

"I know how you feel. Me and Nae still on fucked up terms too."

"Yeah? Your girl is crazy!" she giggled thinking back to the party.

"Yeah I know. I guess I should've warned you."

"Yeah, you should've. But let me go up in here and get something to eat."

"Yeah me too," Marco said even though he wasn't ready for the conversation to end. He wanted to say so much more, but what was there to say? He had to let her go and focus on his family the same as she. Farrah was in an ocean of emotions herself which was why she wanted to end the conversation.

"Marco?"

"Yeah?"

"I just want you to know that I really don't blame you for any of the drama. We both know that this was playing with fire and we both played our parts in it."

"I agree, but it's good to know you feel that way. Thanks for saying it."

"Take care."

"You too."

When Farrah hung up, she was walking into a deli with the silliest smile of on her face until she caught herself and scanned to the room to see if anybody noticed. *Why was it so hard for them to stop liking each other so much? Why couldn't they stay mad at each other for any period of time? Why couldn't they just grow distant already?*

"Jesus!" She said aloud mad at her heart for not following her mind's directions. She wanted to hate Marco and hold a grudge, but that just wasn't her reality.

Chapter 22

Marco's minor brush with the law was a major wake-up call for him. He realized no matter how much he loved Farrah; he needed Nae in his life. Being with Nae and his daughter was what had kept him off the streets and out of trouble. Besides that, he needed her, because she was the only one that would help keep his mind off of Farrah. He convinced himself that he had to be with Nae for Mariah's sake even if deep down inside he wanted Farrah.

For Marco, Nae would always feel like a substitute for the real thing, like a pronoun. He loved Nae, but his love for Farrah somehow went deeper. It was unfair for all parties involved in this twisted monstrosity of lies and deceit. And what was he about to do now? Create an even bigger web of lies.

Marco decided to buy an engagement ring with the money he won at the casino and proposed to Nae. He knew it was what she really wanted, and it would allow him to string her along for years to come, and everyone would be happy for the time being. He showed up at her place unannounced and called her from the driveway.

"Hello?" Nae answered.

"Hey, I'm outside, can you come let me in?"

"What are you doing outside?" Nae asked suspiciously.

"I got something to say, but I need to say it face to face."

"Like what? What's this about?"

"Can you just come let me in?"

"Marco you bet not be on no bullshit, I'm not even in the mood."

"I'm not, I promise. Can you just come open the door?" Marco persisted.

"Alright, I'm coming."

Marco stood on the porch waiting for Nae and feeling nervous about the execution of his fake proposal. Nae looked good when she showed up at the door. He wondered again what stopped him from loving her the way he used to as he stepped inside.

"You looking amazing today," he complimented.

Nae blushed slightly.

"You starting with the BS already huh?"

"What? I can't give you a compliment?"

"Sure, if it was only that simple."

"Whatever, what my daughter doing?"

"She went with my mama to the grocery store," Nae said as she took a seat on the sofa.

"That's kinda good because I wanted to talk to you alone."

"Why you wanna talk to me alone, Marco?"

"Because this is serious business, and I need your undivided attention," he explained as he sat down across from her.

"I'm listening."

"Good."

Nae tried to wait out the pregnant pause, but it seemed to last forever.

"Okay?" she said getting irritated.

Marco took a deep breath.

"Being with you changed my life forever. You gave me a reason to live and a purpose when you gave me my daughter. I know I haven't been even close to the perfect man, but I'm willing to fight for what I love dearly. I could never see myself with someone else, and I could never see me letting this opportunity slip away."

He pulled out the small, dark blue, velvet box and got down on one knee in front of her. Nae's eyes grew big as dinner plates as she slapped her hand over her mouth in amazement. "I know you thought I would never get serious about us. If this ain't serious, I don't know what is. Let's be a family forever," Marco said as he opened the box and the one karat diamond rock blinged brightly leaving Nae completely stunned.

"Marco?" she managed as tears swelled in her eyes.

"Will you marry me Nae?"

The tears came trickling down Nae's face as the reality of his words settled in. The fact that he had done this all on his own with absolutely no pressure from her meant everything to her. It made her feel as if this was really what he wanted. It was definitely all she ever wanted. That moment felt like one of the happiest moments of her life.

"Yes, I will marry you," she cried as she grabbed him by the back of his head and kissed him like never before. She then hugged him so tightly Marco could feel everything she felt in that moment. He was glad to finally be living up to the man she wanted him to be, at least for now. Oddly enough, he felt that what he was doing was the right thing.

****

Raheem had been out of work now for over a month. He filed for unemployment and was denied for reasons neither he nor Farrah understood. There was constant tension in the house and Raheem had reverted back to his old habit of cigar smoking, which Farrah hated. With car notes, insurance, mortgage, and utilities to pay the load was all falling on Farrah. When she paid their life insurance policies for the month it left her with barely enough money for gas. Farrah didn't complain one bit. She knew that in a relationship there would be times when one or the other had to step up to the plate.

What was much more frustrating was the constant accusations and growing jealous rage that Raheem was carrying around. Farrah couldn't leave the house without Raheem calling to see where she was and when she was coming back. If she took too long, he would drive to wherever she claimed to be just to make sure she was really there. He constantly made excuses not to watch Raheem Jr. so Farrah would have to take him everywhere she went. The trust was ruined and for that Farrah accepted the blame, but there was something else going on. The inner workings of an unsettled mind with too much time was the devil's playground.

Raheem's confidence was diminishing and Farrah believed as his woman, it was her job to uplift him when he was down. She cooked his favorite dinner and really put her foot in the homemade macaroni and cheese. She fixed his plate, ran his bath water and made plans to have mind blowing sex once her son went to sleep. She came in the bathroom while Raheem was still drying off from his bath. She was wearing her lace slip-dress bra set while she could still fit into it.

"Give me a kiss," she ordered.

Raheem gave her a small peck, not responding to her lingerie the way she had expected. "Let me see this," she said as she took the towel from his hands and folded it to use as a cushion for her knees. Farrah dropped down on one knee and took his rod into her hand stroking it slowly. She glanced up at him briefly only to find an irritated scowl on his face.

"Baby, I'm not really in the mood tonight," Raheem admitted sending her heart sinking low.

Raheem never rejected her, and being that they hadn't had sex in almost two weeks, his response was baffling. Still, she hid her emotions and tried to be understanding to the situation. Farrah stood up and wrapped her arms around him.

"Baby, I know this is a stressful time, but we will get through it. I believe in you, and I know you will find something soon, just be patient."

"Thanks, baby. I love you," Raheem said.

"I love you too."

She kissed Raheem again and left the bathroom feeling somewhat undesirable and sad.

****

Marco spent the entire weekend with Nae and Mariah, and they had a ball. They went to the movies, The Game Room and Laser Tag. When he arrived at work Monday morning he noticed Farrah wearing a long face when she came in. Throughout the day her somber appearance remained. Something was obviously wrong with her, and it saddened Marco to the point that he felt obligated to reach out to her. He knew he was one of the only people she would talk to about personal matters, and if there was something he could do, she wouldn't even have to ask. He sent her a text on lunch break.

Marco: He can I call you right quick?

Farrah: Yeah

He called her and they went through the normal pleasantries, but Marco could tell something was really bothering her by the burdened tone in her voice.

"I can tell that something is wrong with you, what's going on?" Marco inquired.

"Huuuuuuh," Farrah released. "Everything man."

"Did something happen?"

"Just a lot of stressful stuff going on. He don't have a job, so everything is falling on me. The little money we had in the bank is gone already, bills steady coming in, and I'm just feeling overwhelmed right now. I don't even think I have enough gas in my car to make it through the week. And to make matters even worse, my man don't even wanna fuck me."

"Seriously?"

"Yes, he just seemed like he's turning into a different person right now because that's a problem we never had, no matter what we was going through."

"You mean not having sex?"

"Yeah."

"Damn...I don't even know what to say. If you need a few dollars for gas, though..."

"No, I'll be okay. I appreciate you checking on me. I really do."

"I still care about you, regardless of how things turned out."

"I still care about you too," Farrah admitted.

"Try not to get too down about everything. Remember life is always changing, it never stays the same. Good times will come back around."

"You're right, I know things will get better."

"If you need me, I'm here."

"I have your number wedged in my memory bank," Farrah tittered.

****

When Farrah's call with Marco was over, for some odd reason her spirit was lifted, even though nothing had changed. It was like whenever he was around, everything was just fine. She shook her head knowing it was terrible that he had that effect on her. Just knowing he was always there for her gave her some much-needed peace of mind at the moment. She was enjoying the last of a shrimp and french fry dinner sitting in the parking lot in her jeep when she looked

169

up and spotted Marco headed in her direction. Thirty minutes had passed since their conversation and she just looked on wondering was he really coming to her.

She looked around to see who was all outside, and who was lurking in the shadows. They hadn't been seen together in over a month and it was scary. As he approached her driver's side she rolled the window down. Marco produced a small envelope and passed it to her.

"I saw this card while I was out and it just made me think of us."

As Farrah took the card in her hand, Marco walked away before she could even respond. Farrah wiped her hands on a nearby napkin and opened the envelope. The card on the inside was a guy and a girl with their arms around each other's shoulders and their heads tilted towards one another. The front of the card read *Friendship*. When she opened the car a hundred dollar bill fell out onto her lap.

"Oh my God," she said aloud as a big smile spread across her face. Even though she had refused his help, Marco had forced a small blessing upon her, and she couldn't deny that it was right on time. She looked at the inside of the card that read *Real Friends Last Forever*. The gesture coupled with the way she felt about him at the moment made her eyes swell with tears and she blinked them away. Before heading back to work she sent him and simple text of appreciation.

Farrah: Thank you so much

Marco: Anytime

Just then, she saw Kevin walk by seemingly out of nowhere with the most sinister grin on his face. She didn't think much of it, but it was funny how he was always popping up out of the blue.

Chapter 23

In the following weeks, Farrah continued to struggle financially as well as personally. Her and Raheem's sex life wasn't even half of what it used to be, and she began to wonder was he cheating on her. Once she rationalized, the thought left as quickly as it came. Raheem was a good man, and she was sure of that. Marco continued to help out Farrah here and there. Even though she felt guilty for accepting his help, it gave her some solace that he wanted nothing in return. They continued to keep their distance, for the most part, knowing what was at stake for the both of them. They had small chats once weekly, and during that time if Marco felt the need, he would pass her a card with money inside.

Still, it was hard for her seeing Marco every day and not being around him the way she was accustomed to. She started having dreams again of the two of them together, and it only made the time they were together at work feel more like torture sometimes. Some days, she just watched him walk by and would vision herself walking up tongue kissing him long and hard, but she never let on to him the way she was feeling. On the days when Raheem was distant and unaffectionate she'd find herself in the shower masturbating with the shower head to thoughts of Marco.

One day, they spotted each other at the mall and both were with their families. Nae noticed Farrah, but she could tell Raheem did not see Marco and she thanked God for that. He was still being overly possessive and that kept Farrah in check about acting on her hidden desire to be with Marco. It was appealing to see Marco being a family man and she believed he would be a good man to her if she wasn't already taken. One day, after the day at the mall, Farrah walked in on Raheem going through her phone obviously looking for signs of infidelity.

"What the fuck? Man, you outta control!" she insisted.

"What you scared of?" Raheem accused as he fingered through her phone. "You scared I'm a find something?"

Farrah had memorized Marco's number long ago and always deleted any conversations they had so she wasn't the least bit concerned about him finding something.

"I ain't scared of shit, ain't nothing to find."

"You acting like it."

"That's not the point. Do I go through your phone?"

Raheem took his phone and toss it on the bed.

"Go ahead, you ain't gon' find nothing," he assured her.

Farrah took the phone and began to go through the contacts and text messages just out of spite, knowing she wouldn't find anything and she was right. Raheem's phone was always dry as a bone since he'd been off work. Even his closest friends rarely ever called him anymore to hanging since he was broke. Farrah continued to go through his phone and his social media pages secretly hoping to find something incriminating that would give her a reason to do what she really wanted to do. Even as Raheem was breathing down her neck with suspicions she still could not shake her growing desire. No matter how much she loved Raheem she just could not seem to wash Marco off her skin.

****

Marco celebrated his first birthday as a free man by hanging out downtown clubbing with friends and ended the night at an after-hours strip club call Déjà-vu. Nae was a little disappointed he didn't choose to spend the day with her, but for the past few weeks he'd been the perfect man to her, so she didn't fight him on it. He had to pat himself on the back for being able to simultaneously keep a smile on Nae and Farrah's faces. He woke up the next morning in his apartment and realized it was almost noon. He still had a huge boner from all the lap dances that ended his night. He shook his head thinking, *what a night,* as he rolled out of bed to take a leak.

When he came from the bathroom the message alert was lighting up on his phone. The massage came in from an unsaved contact and he knew it was Farrah.

Farrah: You busy?

Marco: Not at all

Farrah: You sure? I don't need no more drama, and you don't either.

Marco: You good.

Seconds later his phone rang, and he quickly answered with a smile on his face.

"What's up?"

"Hey birthday boy! How you feeling?"

"I'm feeling good."

"Happy belated. I would have reached out yesterday, but I figured you was with her."

"It's cool. I actually hung out with my homies."

"Yeah? No hangover or nothing?"

"Naw, I'm good. How you doing?"

"How am I doing? I'm horny," Farrah admitted.

"What?" Marco chuckled in shock.

Farrah was all alone at home at the time, and she had decided if she couldn't be with Marco she would settle for the next best thing.

"You know what I want?"

"What you want baby? Tell daddy."

"I want you to handle this pussy like only you can."

"You miss this pound game huh?" Marco said feeling like the man.

"I do...I got my panties down around my ankles and I'm just stroking myself, thinking about that pound game."

Marco caught on quickly to what was happening as he grabbed his boxers and started stroking his rod.

"I been fiending for that pussy too. I'm a get me some peaches and grapes and go to work."

"Yes, daddy! I want that. I want all that," Farrah admitted as she fingered herself.

"You can get it. You can get this dick from the back, the long way...all night baby."

"I want you to cuff me to the bed and destroy this pussy."

Marco envisioned himself in the process with a hand full of himself stroking away.

"What else you want baby? Tell daddy what else you want?"

"I want you to spank this ass until it turn red."

"I'm a put my name on."

"Mmmm," Farrah moaned as she began to heat up. "You already did."

"Oh yeah? Who's is it then? Tell me who's it is."

"It's yours. It's yours! Oh shit! Oooh, Oh shit!" Farrah shouted as she began to finger herself until she squirted all over her bed sheets and Marco bust off into a pillow case.

"Got damn! Hold on," Marco said as he finished bussing one long amazing nut then strips naked knowing he needed to go straight to the shower.

"Hello?" He heard Farrah say.

"Yeah I'm here. Shit girl, where the hell did all that come from?"

"It's been building up inside of me the entire time."

"I know me too. What we gon' do about this situation?"

"I don't know, I'm just lost right now. At least I got that out of my system for a minute."

"Ha! Glad I could help."

"Let me go before this crazy man comes back."

"Alright."

"Still love you."

"Still love you too baby."

Marco hung up from Farrah and just sat butt naked on the bed wondering what just happened. The only thing he knew for sure was that after that phone sex stunt she just pulled it would be no stopping him from pursuing her now. He knew now that she wanted this dangerous love affair just as much as he did.

****

Monday morning came, and Marco was excited to return to work, knowing he would get to see Farrah. Once again, she began to consume his thoughts and he got that overwhelming feeling that he just had to have her. The day started off smoothly for the most part, but then Kevin began with his bullshit, piling extra work on Marco for no apparent reason. Being a team player, he didn't complain, he just did what he was told to do. His thoughts weren't exactly focused on the day to day grind at the moment.

Just as things were slowing down and going back to normal, Kevin popped up at his station.

"Aye, I need you to come work the back line for a minute," Kevin explained

"Damn Kevin, you can't get somebody else? I worked three lines today already."

"It's a busy day today, what you want me to say?"

"I want you to say I'm not the only nigga in here that know how to work these lines."

Kevin looked at Marco as if he was appalled.

177

"I mean, really, niggas should be glad to just have a job fresh out of jail. You know how hard it is to find a job right now?"

Kevin was throwing it back up in his face that he had done him a big favor, getting him a job when he really needed one. That truth was something Marco never denied. Kevin did look out for him, even if he was being a bitch about it now.

"Whatever man, what you need me to do?" Marco finally said as Kevin took off and Marco followed. He went to the back line, and now he was working right across from Farrah. They could see each other from a distance. They exchanged subtle glances here and there and she smiled at him once. Marco's burning desire for Farrah was like nothing he'd ever known. Today his desire was distracting him from his building frustration with Kevin. When the line stopped and he had to restock, he saw Farrah walk away in the direction of the restrooms. He waited for a moment then he took off in the same direction.

As he rounded the break room he saw Farrah coming out of the women's restroom. He quickly grabbed her hand and pulled her behind a vending machine where no one could see them. Without hesitation, he palmed her ass and stuck his tongue in her mouth. She accepted his tongue and offered her own in return. When their lip lock was broken Farrah made a motion to head back to her station, but Marco held her in place.

"You know you can't just fuck my head up like that and leave it there."

"Marco it's hard. I can't just get away like I used to. He be one me for every little thing."

"I know, but if there's a will there's a way."

"You gon' get us in trouble again."

Marco ran his hand through her long brown hair.

"No, I'm not. We gon' play it safe I promise."

"We should get back to work before someone realizes we're both missing."

She tried to leave again.

"First promise me you'll get away. I need you, Farrah," he said kissing her neck. "I need you and I know you need me."

"Okay, okay. I promise I'll find a way to come and be with you."

Marco could feel her little baby bump starting to grow as he pressed up against her. Her breasts were fuller and her skin was glowing.

"I wanna fuck you right here and now," he admitted.

"Calm down soldier. Just make sure you have my fruit bowl ready."

He smacked her on her booty as he left.

"Gon' get back to work," Marco added.

Chapter 24

Marco, Nae, and Mariah were all lying in bed together watching the sequel to the kids' movie *Are We There Yet?* Mariah lay at the foot of the bed, glued to the flat screen while Marco and Nae snuggled up together. These were the times Marco cherished the most, and he understood why him being there meant so much to Nae and Mariah. Hidden under a cozy blanket, Marco's hands roamed under Nae's dress caressing her soft, brown skin.

"Bae?" Nae spoke in a low tone.

"What?"

"What would you say if I said I was pregnant?"

Marco was frozen stiff by her words. Mariah's head spun around out of curiosity. Marco sat up in the bed.

"What do you mean?"

"I'm not pregnant okay, Mariah?" Nae said wiggling her neck and signaling for Mariah to go back to watching television. Marco relaxed back under the cover.

"Oh, don't scare me like that."

"I just wanted to know if it happened, how you would feel about it, I guess."

"Ummm."

"You gave me your answer already."

"Nae, you ain't never said nothing about wanting no more kids."

"And I didn't say that just now either, did I?"

"Why you getting defensive?"

"It was just a question. I wanted to know because it could happen if I don't hurry up and get back on some form of birth control."

"I didn't know you wasn't."

"I just told you that the other night, but I should have known you were drunk cause you said..."

Nae paused realizing her daughter could hear her. "Never mind, the point is it could happen because we're both young healthy adults."

"We'll, I'm not in a rush to have no more kids if we being honest. I like giving all me time and attention to my little munching. Ain't that right, Mariah?"

"Huh?" Mariah said when she heard her name.

"Don't try to act like you wasn't listening," Marco said.

"Oh yeah, I don't want no sisters," Mariah said.

"What about a brother?" Nae suggested.

Mariah pondered over the question for a moment, but could not reach a definite decision.

"I don't know."

Marco and Nae went back to spooning and watching the movie as he stroked her hair with his free hand.

"So, about this wedding date..." Nae said.

After his proposal, Marco and Nae agreed to wait until he was off parole to set a date for the wedding. Now she was all of sudden talking about a date.

"I thought we agreed to wait until I get off papers?"

"Yeah, but I mean, you only got about nine months left. I don't see no harm in setting a date."

Marco's eyes roamed around in his head. Lucky for him, Nae had her back to him because she would have surely been tipped off by his demeanor that he wasn't really ready.

"I just wanna wait until I'm completely done with the Michigan Department of Corrections."

"Just to set a date?"

"Yeah," Marco said in an irritated tone.

Nae sighed.

"I don't understand."

"Okay, well, can we just watch the movie and talk about it another time?"

Nae lay quietly in bed as her mind wandered. The last thing she wanted to do was ruin a chill day with drama, but it was something on her mind that had to be said and it had to be said now. She paused the movie on Netflix.

"Mariah, go to your room for a minute, we'll finish watching the movie in a second."

As soon as Marco heard her tone, he knew the hammer was about to drop. When Nae sounded extremely calm, it usually meant she was trying to defuse her anger and keep her emotions from rising.

"Here we go again," Marco said as Mariah left the room.

"Ain't no here we go again."

"Okay, what you tell Mariah to leave for?"

"Listen…on some real, real, real shit. I'm not the same young dumb girl you had wrapped all around your fingers at eighteen."

"Who said you was?"

"If you really don't want this, don't play with my heart."

"If I didn't want it, I wouldn't have bought a ring and proposed Nae."

"Right, so don't make me feel like I'm pressuring you into some shit. All I'm asking for is to set a date. Planning a wedding takes time."

Marco's plan sounded much better in his head than it was turning out in reality. Trapped in the bedroom with no escape route he had two choices; keep it real or keep it going. He chose the latter.

"If setting a date is what's gonna make this real for you, then let's set a date."

Nae looked into his eyes and Marco didn't blink. She knew he loved her. She could only hope that he really wanted to spend the rest of his life with her. They set a date and managed to salvage the rest of the evening without conflict. As the hours passed Marco begin to rationalize his decision. If it came down to it, being married to the mother of his child didn't seem so bad, even though he knew that wasn't the way he should feel about marriage. He knew deep down that a trip to the alter wouldn't keep him from Farrah. The only thing that could keep him from Farrah was Farrah. If he had his way they'd keep creeping around for the rest of their natural lives.

****

Farrah had been trying every trick in the book to get away from Raheem and her son long enough to go spend some time with Marco, but nothing worked. Even when she went to the salon, Raheem would claim he need to borrow her jeep so he could drop her off and pick her up. When she asked to drive his car he'd claim there was no gas in it, knowing she wouldn't want to spend the extra money.

The fact that she even had money for the salon was an issue that caused arguments on more than one occasion. But Marco was a man that knew how to keep her smiling in and out of the bedroom, and for that, she believed he deserves what he was asking for. She was going to make it happen, one way or another. She feared there would soon come a time when she'd gain weight and become less attractive, but for now, Marco still made her feel like the sexiest woman in the world.

Finally, out of all options, Farrah devised the only feasible plan that wasn't a safety hazard for the both of them. They wouldn't have much time, but if she knew Marco he would definitely make the most of it. One morning Farrah woke up extra early for work. While Raheem was in a deep sleep she got dressed and slipped her handcuffs in her purse. She left for work thirty minutes earlier than normal, but instead of heading to the job, she detoured to Marco's apartment. When she arrived, Marco was grinning with anticipation. She walked in moving at a no-nonsense pace. She took the handcuffs from her purse and passed them to Marco as she began to undress on her way to the bedroom.

****

Marco and Farrah managed to barely make it to work on time, pulling in the lot right behind each other, still feeling the high of their thirty-minute fuck session. The two of them entered the lobby laughing and whispering about all the freaky things that had just transpired. When they walked out onto the main floor they were still caught up in the moment and Kevin zeroed in on the bonding.

"Aye Marco, I need you at your station we about to get started," Kevin said.

Marco's smile turned upside down quickly.

"I'm on my way there now, I know what time we start," he shot back.

"Why he always acting like a braud?" Farrah whispered.

"You know why," Marco assured her as they parted ways and headed to their stations.

As Marco glanced back at Kevin he could see the malice in his eyes. He couldn't understand why Kevin hated him so much over Farrah, but the feeling was now mutual. As the day progress, Marco couldn't help but think of how his friendship with Kevin had deteriorated. He wondered how much longer it would be before things came to a head, and they had a serious altercation.

Shortly after, he looked up and noticed Kevin hanging out at Farrah's station. Kevin wasn't her supervisor, so he wondered what it was about. The two were engaged in a giggly conversation that caused a hint of jealousy to run through Marco's blood. As the conversation continued, he realized that was exactly what Kevin wanted to accomplish. He realized that this battle had already been won long ago and there was no need to sweat Kevin. Still, almost thirty minutes later he was still at her station hanging out, and no matter how much he didn't want to admit it, Kevin's plan was starting to work.

"It look like your boy over there trying to get on," Kiara said.

"I see," Marco responded calmly.

When he was finally finished flirting with Farrah, Kevin made sure to stroll by Marco's workstation wearing a sinister grin as if he'd accomplished something. It was one thing to dislike someone, but to constantly work at pushing their buttons was something different. By the time lunch was near and Kevin popped up his station, Marco had already realized that today could be the day their tension came to a head.

"We sending some people on second shift, they backed up again, so I need you to help out,' Kevin informed.

"Naw, I'm not going back on second shift, find somebody else," Marco said with certainty in his tone.

"Whatchu mean? You refusing to work?"

"I'm refusing to work second shift nigga!"

"Hold on. Why every time I ask you to do something it's a problem?"

Marco was fed up with the cat and mouse games and tired of not addressing the real issues.

"Truthfully, you been on some real gay shit for a while now. Talking behind my back, sending me on second shift, when you got five other niggas that can do it and been here less time than me. I know what this is about; it's all about that girl. But let me tell you something. You could fire me right now and never see me again, and she still wouldn't fuck with you, so I'm not your problem. You know why? Because I'm real man, and you just a bitch ass nigga with a title."

Kevin's blood was boiling. He couldn't believe how Marco was talking him so he snapped.

"Nigga fuck you and that bitch. If it wasn't for me, your punk ass would probably be in prison right now. I'm not asking you, I'm telling you; you going back to second shift, bitch ass nigga!"

Marco went from seeing all his coworkers around him, to just seeing a blank redness everywhere. When he found Kevin's face, he punched him in it, sending him stumbling backward down a small staircase. Marco jumped down the staircase and pounce on him immediately with three swift blows to both sides of Kevin's jaw.

Kevin managed to grab Marco in a headlock that allowed him some time to recover. He started punching Marco in the head repeatedly until Marco found his stomach and bit into it like a steak.

"Ahhhhh!" Kevin screamed as he released Marco and took off running up the floor. Marco tried to go after him, but was held back by some more supervisors and coworkers.

"I'm a fuck you up boy, this ain't over," Marco yelled out to Kevin.

The head supervisor walked up to Marco.

"Punch out and go home right now," he ordered.

Everyone stood around in complete shock of what had just happened. Marco knew without anyone saying it that he'd just lost his job. To him, it was almost worth it just to get his hands on Kevin. As he stormed to the time clock he could see Farrah standing on her table watching him. He blamed her at the moment for everything that happened. Maybe he should have just listened to Kevin in the first place and left her alone.

Chapter 25

Farrah called Marco as soon as she went to lunch, but he didn't answer. She continued to call him having major concerns about his frame of mind at the moment. He finally answered.

"What?" he yelled into the phone.

"Why you yelling at me? I'm just trying to make sure you're okay."

"I'm okay, now what?"

Farrah didn't understand why he was lashing out at her.

"Are you upset with me Marco?"

"This shit is all your fucking fault," he accused.

"My fault? How is it my fault?"

"I just don't understand how a nigga could hold a grudge over something he never had."

Marco wasn't thinking rational anymore. In his mind he believed there had to be more to the story that Farrah wasn't telling him about her and Kevin.

"I don't know what you trying to say, but that shit sound stupid as hell. If I had ever mess with Kevin ain't no way in hell I would've ever fucked with you. You know me better than that."

Marco was so frustrated at the time, he just needed a target to release his anger and Farrah was available.

"And what the fuck was you and him talking about all day?"

"It wasn't all day, and it wasn't about nothing. He was just telling me a funny fucking story that's all," she shot back getting angry now.

Farrah began to realize she was being interrogated and attacked for no good reason. She got enough of that from Raheem and she didn't need it from Marco too.

"You know what? I just need to be left alone right now so I can clear my head," Marco surmised.

"Fine!" Farrah shouted before hanging up.

She was pissed that she wanted to be there for Marco like he was always there for her, but instead he was attacking her character. It was becoming more and more overwhelming to constantly try and please two men, but her heart was divided between them.

****

That same afternoon Marco received a call from the job confirming his termination. Once he had time to calm down, he was just thankful no one decided to get the police involved. An assault charge would have been in major violation of his parole. He tried to explain to Nae the reason he was fired, but it was hard to relay the conflict between he and Kevin without the missing component, which was Farrah. Marco made it sound as if the entire fallout was about Marco not wanting to work second shift, but Nae could tell there was more to the story.

Eventually, he apologized to Farrah and they made up in less than a week. Marco realized that although Farrah was the source of the problem, he couldn't blame her for his own actions. With no onsite communication Marco and Farrah had to resort back to phone calls and text messages, but that was nowhere near as easy nowadays. Nae accused Marco of having something to hide because his phone was never out in the open like hers. They had big fights about it that would land him back at his apartment waiting out the storm.

The conflict with Nae allowed him the opportunity to see and spend time with Farrah. She came to see him again one early morning and they had a quickie sex session before she went to work. She promised she would take a sick day from work without telling Raheem and she would come and spend the day with him. Marco was really looking forward to her sick day. Since the beginning of their love affair they hadn't spent more than an hour or two alone together. Unlike Raheem, Marco was approved for his unemployment which took a lot of stress from his situation.

His main focus became the women in his life and the position he played in theirs. When the day came for Farrah to play hooky from work, she was their bright and early as promised. It was late November and the snow had made its debut overnight, spreading a thin white layer on the ground. It was so early the first thing they did was lay down and went back to sleep. Holding Farrah in his arms as he dozed in and out of consciousness was a unique and enjoyable experience. It was weird to be cuddled up with a woman who was pregnant with another man's baby, but Marco rationalize his actions with the knowing that the baby's father was still in question. When they awoke they had passionate sex and then kissed and cuddled and laughed the hours away.

Farrah made them breakfast food in the afternoon and they sat in the living room feeding their faces.

"So how are things at home now?" Marco finally asked.

"Better I guess. We don't bump heads as much as we was doing."

"Good."

"He supposed to have a job interview today."

"I hope so because my bank gon' be closed for a minute," Marco joked, but not really.

"Shut up nigga," she punched his arm. "I never asked you to do all that stuff."

"I know. That's what makes me wanna do it because you never asked."

Farrah released a happy sigh. Just being in Marco's presence made her feel good.

"It feels strange loving two men."

"It feels strange loving two women. But at least we don't have to choose."

"Thank God," Farrah said relieved she didn't have that pressure on her head at the moment. "Let me ask you something, hypothetically speaking."

"Okay."

"If I were to ever break up with Raheem, do you think you would want to be with me? Do you think I would make a good woman?"

It was something Marco had often fantasized about, but his fantasy was better than reality.

"I mean, I could ask you the same thing, but since you asked first, I'll be honest. First off I think you would

192

make any man a great woman. It would be extremely hard to turn down the chance to have you all to myself, but there's something I haven't told you, and I probably won't get a better chance than this."

"What's that?" Farrah said as her heart rate increased.

"Me and Nae are engaged."

Farrah stared blankly at the wall in front of her for a while then started blinking her eyes repeatedly. She was trying to process the information. It felt like a dagger.

"When did this happen?"

"Not long ago."

At first, she was heartbroken and disappointed, but then she began to realize that just like her, Marco needed his family together.

"Congratulations, I guess," Farrah said dryly.

"Don't say it like that. I mean, do you honestly think me and you would stand a chance...hypothetically speaking?"

"I think we would have some major trust issues."

"You damn right," Marco admitted.

"So does this mean you're about to dump me?" Farrah asked.

"Hell naw, I'm not going nowhere. Would you dump me if you got married?"

"No. I don't think I could ever get you out of my system."

"We'll just have to be a lot more careful."

"Right," Farrah agreed.

Marco gave her a peck on the lips.

"I love you girl, don't ever forget it."

"I love you too boy."

They knew their time together was coming to an end as Farrah closed out her false eight-hour shift. "I really enjoyed you today."

"I enjoyed you more," Marco said. "Especially that bomb ass pussy."

"Ha! It's yours whenever you want it," Farrah said as she stood up and searched for her things.

Farrah got dress and Marco walked her outside.

"I hope I see you again soon."

"Maybe not real soon. You know I can't be taking days off, but we'll always find a way."

"Damn right."

As they made their way down the steps and out to the parking lot neither one of them spotted the red Charger in the lot until it started up, taking off in their direction. Farrah was frozen in shock and her mouth couldn't form any words as she peered inside at Raheem behind the wheel. She managed to formulate four words just in time.

"Oh shit, that's Raheem!"

Just then Raheem jumped the curb onto the sidewalk and hopped out the car with a gun in his hand. Marco feared for his and Farrah's life. Raheem had a fire in his eyes that was non-negotiable.

"Didn't I tell you what was gon' happen if I caught you cheating bitch?"

"Raheem please just calm down," Farrah begged as he approached gripping the steel.

At first, Marco stood bravely in front of Farrah trying to protect her, but as he saw the rage in this mad man's eyes, he realized he couldn't take a bullet for Farrah, no matter how much he loved her. He realized he had a child to live for, and he threw his hands up in surrender as he backed away slowly. As Raheem maintained eye contact with him Marco quickly realized Raheem wasn't there for Farrah's life, he was there for his. As he raised the gun Marco spun around and ran for dear life.

The exploding sound of the first gunshot skipped his heart beat for a second as the bullet ripped through the side of his puffy coat without striking him. More shots rang out as he darted up the steps with his would-be assassin in hot pursuit. As he reached the second floor, Marco realized he'd left his door slightly cracked open knowing he wasn't leaving the house. Another shot rang out as he scrambled inside ducked down so low, he landed on all fours, slamming the door behind him. His heart pounded like never before as he dashed through the house in a panic. He heard banging at the door.

"Don't run nigga, come out here and face me like a man!" Raheem screamed outside.

Marco lifted his mattress and grabbed his 40 Glock. He had been in a few gun battles in his life, and he wasn't about to back down from this one. If Raheem wanted a gun fight he was going to get it.

"Come on muthafucka!" he barked as he racked the gun and put a bullet in the chamber.

Farrah caught up with Raheem and even as she feared for her own life, she begged Raheem to stop pursuing Marco. Raheem had no chill at this point. He had already seen enough evidence to know he was being played. Raheem didn't have a job interview. It was just an excuse to get up early so he could follow Farrah's moves. He had been following her around since he notices she was leaving out for work way too early. One day, he parked near her job and discreetly followed Marco home from work. When he realized Farrah's jeep wasn't at her job, he knew exactly where to look for her.

"Shut the fuck up bitch, I told you don't try to play me," Raheem barked as he began kicking on the door until it finally came open.

"Raheem Nooooooo!" Farrah screamed as he forced his way inside.

Raheem walked right into a death trap as Marco stood in the center of the room, locked and loaded. As soon as he had Raheem in full view, he fired three rounds. Raheem's big frame stumbled backwards as each bullet tagged him in chest ripping through organs. His body dropped right at the threshold of the front door. All Marco could hear was Farrah's frantic cries for help outside his door. His adrenaline was on overload as he stood in the living room with the smoking gun in his hand. Farrah appeared in the doorway kneeling over Raheem's lifeless body, sobbing uncontrollably. It was in that moment Raheem was able to process just what he'd done.

Chapter 26

Marco was taking into custody on the scene. He knew he was going back to prison just for being a felon in possession of a firearm alone. He could only hope that the truth would come out in court that he was really just defending himself, with no other options available. He was immediately hit with a parole hold which meant it didn't matter what his bond was because he wasn't going anywhere. He had to fight the case in the county jail, back living with the riffraff, hustlers and fiends. For a long time he wouldn't accept visits from Nae. How could he ever explain what had happened? After a couple of months Nae gave up. Farrah was subpoenaed to testify in court, and when she took the stand, to Marco's surprise she told the jury everything exactly the way it happened.

Her testimony made her look like a bad person, and she cried on the stand. She put all the blame on herself and the stress of it all caused her to have a miscarriage eighteen weeks into her pregnancy. Before the trial ended Marco was offered a plea deal of six years for manslaughter and felony firearm. He had been in the county for almost a year and he knew he was headed back to prison regardless. Knowing he was responsible for taking a man's life, he took the deal. It was another nine months before he received any words from Nae or Farrah. Ironically, both the letters arrived on the same day.

It took Marco hours to gather the courage to open either letter. He waited to later that night and opened Nae's letter first.

Dear Marco, I received all your letters, but I haven't read them. After watching everything play out in court there was really nothing left to say. You proposed to me knowing you were in love with another woman, and for that, I will never forgive you. I only wish you could be here to help me raise the child we created. You've already missed out on so many important moments in her life, and you're about to miss out on a lot more. I help her read the letters you write to her and will continue to do so.

I just wish I would have seen you for who you really were sooner because I could've saved myself a lot of heartache and pain. I'm just writing you to let you know that I've met someone new. If things do work out, he will become a part of Mariah's life as well. It's sad to think that someone else could end up playing the part that you were so good at.

The letter felt like a brick in the chest the way it ended so harshly and abruptly. It was almost like an intentional dagger through the heart adding on the fact that another man could end up raising his daughter. Knowing he had another tough pill to swallow her hurriedly opened Farrah's letter and took a deep breath.

Dear Marco, it took me so long to sit down and write this only letter to you. I want you to know that although I don't blame you, I could never, ever forgive you. You took my son's father away from him and that's something I'll have to live with the rest of my life. One day, you will come home and have a chance to be a part of your daughter's life again, but my son won't ever have that opportunity. As you may know, I lost the baby due to all the overwhelming circumstances. It was probably for the best because my gut tells me that was your baby. As much as I still love you, I wish we never met. Our lives would be so much different and better right now had we never became friends.

Maybe we should have just quit when we had the chance. I've asked myself a million times how did I get so wrapped up into something so wrong. My only answer is always the same; it felt right at the time. Please do not try and contact me in any way. It's going to take years to free myself of the bond we created and the heartache it caused. I wish you the best.

Farrah

If he wasn't in prison surrounded by a bunch of hardened criminals Marco would have surely let the tears fall that he was holding back. In a very short time, he had established something so real that he couldn't see life any other way. There was no way he could have ever imagined a life without Farrah or Nae in it, but that's exactly what he was facing now. As he sat and reminisced, he thought about the line in the movie *Bronx Tale* when Sonny tells the kid he would only get a few special women in a lifetime. He knew for a fact he'd had at least two of them and for that reason, he still didn't regret Farrah, even with all she had cost him. Farrah was like a dream come true, and fantasy turned into a reality that brought him unprecedented happiness. Now he had almost five years hard time left to try and wash her off his skin.

Made in the USA
Columbia, SC
14 November 2022

71169219R00111